Harry and the Terrible Whatzit

BY DICK GACKENBACH

Clarion Books/New York

FOR LILA, HELEN, ANNA, AND ARLENE

Clarion Books
a Houghton Mifflin Company imprint
215 Park Avenue South, New York, NY 10003
Text and illustrations copyright © 1977 by Dick Gackenbach

For information about permission to reproduce selections from this book, write to
Permissions, Houghton Mifflin Company,
215 Park Avenue South, New York, NY 10003.

For information about this and other Houghton Mifflin trade and reference books
and multimedia products, visit The Bookstore at Houghton Mifflin on the World
Wide Web at (http://www.hmco.com/trade/).

Printed in the USA.

Library of Congress Cataloging-in-Publication Data

Gackenbach, Dick.
Harry and the terrible whatzit

"A Clarion book."

Summary: When his mother goes to the cellar and doesn't return right away,
Harry goes down to search for her and confronts the terrible two-headed Whatzit.
I. Title.
PZ7.G117Har [E] 76-40205
ISBN 0-395-28795-2   PA ISBN 0-89919-223-8

HOR 30 29 28 27 26 25 24 23 22 21

I knew
there was something terrible
down in the cellar.
I just knew, because
the cellar was dark and damp
and it smelled.

"Don't go down there,"
I told my mother.
"Why?" she asked.
"There is something terrible
down there."

"I have to go down
in the cellar,"
she said.
"We need a jar
of pickles."

She never believes me!

I waited
and
waited
and
waited
at the
cellar door.
She never came back up.

Someone had to do something,
so I took a broom
and went down the cellar steps.
It was
very
black
and
gloomy.
And it smelled.

"I know there is something here,"
I called out.
"What did you do
with my mother?"

Then I saw it!
A double-headed,
three-clawed,
six-toed,
long-horned
Whatzit.

It was hiding
behind the furnace.

"Where is my mother?"
I asked it.
"The last time I saw your mother,"
the Whatzit said,
"she was over by the pickle jars, Runt."

I was sure the Whatzit was lying. "What did you do with her?" I shouted, and I gave it a swat with the broom. WHAM!

That made the Whatzit really mad
and it came after me.

I swung the broom again. WHAM!
The Whatzit didn't like that at all.

It climbed up on the washer
and I hit it right where it sits down.

I noticed the Whatzit was getting smaller.
And when I pulled its tail,
it got even smaller.

16

Now the Whatzit was down to my size.
"Okay, you better tell me what you did
with my mother," I said. "Or else!"
"Kid, you're crazy," the Whatzit answered.
One of the heads made a face at me.

Just for that I twisted a nose,
and the Whatzit shrank some more.
"Why are you getting so small?"
I asked.

"Because you aren't afraid of me anymore," the Whatzit said.
"That always happens just when I'm beginning
 to feel at home in a closet or a cellar."
The Whatzit looked very sad.

The Whatzit
got smaller and
smaller and smaller.
Just when it was
about the size of a peanut,
I called out,
"Try Sheldon Parker's cellar
next door.
He's afraid of everything."
"Thanks," I heard it say.
Then the Whatzit was gone.

The Whatzit disappeared
before it could tell me
what it had done
to my mother.
I looked in the washer.
She was not in there.

I looked
behind some boxes.
My mother
was not there either.

I looked
inside the wood bin.
No mother there.
I was very worried.

Then I found her glasses
beside the pickle jars.
But what had happened
to the rest of her?

I was searching
for more clues
when I discovered
the back cellar door
was open.

24

I looked
outside,
and there
in the
bright sunlight ...

25

… was my mother picking flowers.
Boy, was I glad to see her.

"I found your glasses in the cellar,"
I said.
"Thank you, Harry," she said.
"But I thought you were afraid
of the cellar."
"Not anymore," I answered.
"The terrible Whatzit is gone.
I chased it away with the broom!"

"Well," she said, "*I* never saw a Whatzit down there."
She never believes me.

27

I helped her carry
the pickles into the
kitchen where she
gave me some
milk and cookies.

"You know what, Harry,"
my mother said.
"I will never worry about
a Whatzit as long as
you are around."
Maybe she did believe me.

Later I heard an awful yell
coming from the house next door.
I'll bet Sheldon looked in the cellar.

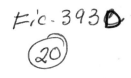

"I know there is
something here,"
I called out.
"What did you do
with my mother?"

Then I saw it!
A double-headed,
three-clawed,
six-toed,
long-horned
Whatzit.

$6.95

ISBN 0-89919-223-8

1-12371

90000

9 780899 192239

DECORATIVE FURNITURE

with DONNA DEWBERRY

DECORATIVE
FURNITURE
with DONNA DEWBERRY

NORTH LIGHT BOOKS
CINCINNATI, OHIO
www.nlbooks.com

06   05   04   03   9   8   7   6

Library of Congress Cataloging-in-Publication Data

Dewberry, Donna S.
    Decorative furniture with Donna Dewberry / Donna Dewberry.
        p. cm.
    Includes bibliographical references and index.
    ISBN 1-58180-016-9 (pbk. : alk. paper) -- ISBN 1-58180-017-7 (alk. paper)
    1. Furniture painting. 2. Decoration and ornament. I. Title.

TT199.4 .D48 2000
745.7'2--dc21
                                                                00-041862

Editor: Kathy Kipp
Interior Design: Angela Wilcox
Interior Production: Ben Rucker
Production Coordinator: Sara Dumford
Photography: Christine Polomsky and Al Parrish

Dedication & Acknowledgments

This book is dedicated to my daughter Maria. I was in the middle of writing another version of this dedication when she passed away on May 5, 2000. Today is May 15th and I think I can write this and make some sense. I need to share with you as many have shared with me through this difficult time. The outpouring of your love and concern has overwhelmed me and my family. My heart is sad this day but there is an equal amount of gladness as I reflect upon Maria and the wonderful memories we have.

Now I must begin this dedication, for just as sure as the sun came up this morning and will each day, I too must go on. Words cannot describe the feelings that have been with me these last few days, but I will attempt to honor Maria with the words that I write.

There are so many things I would like to write about but I will concentrate on what I feel is the most important point Maria made in her life. That point is that we all matter and that no one needs to be left out. She saw the world as a beautiful place and cheered up everyone she encountered. A good example of that was a young man whom she met only once in her apartment building's laundry room. He attended Maria's memorial service in Utah and stood up and spoke for a brief moment, stating that she seemed so special and seemed to light up the room when she came in.

Maria is probably best described in a few lines that one of her best friends wrote to her in a letter: "You're like that paint brush in those black and white cartoons that magically brings color and life to everything in its path, and grass suddenly grows greener and the flowers grow and skies turn blue and the birds start to chirp and sing and the animals all come out to see what has brought all this magical happiness."

So each time I pick up my paint brush, I hope I will be able to paint a little more color into the world as I'm sure Maria would want me to.

Love,
Mom and Dad

I would like to take this opportunity to acknowledge all those who assisted in the production of this book. Thanks go to the following:

Kathy Kipp, my editor at North Light Books, for her hard work, patience and true friendship.

The rest of the North Light family and staff for all the work they do to make a book like this a reality.

My office staff, Maribel and Michelle, who filled in while I worked on this book.

My family, who sacrificed so that I could complete this book.

My fellow painters who have supported me and shared with me. I love each of you and am thankful to have your friendship.

Finally, thanks to my husband, Marc, who loves me in spite of the craziness that goes on while a book like this is completed.

Thanks to each of you.

Donna

Contents

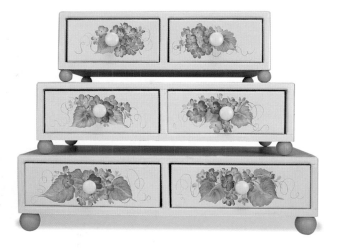

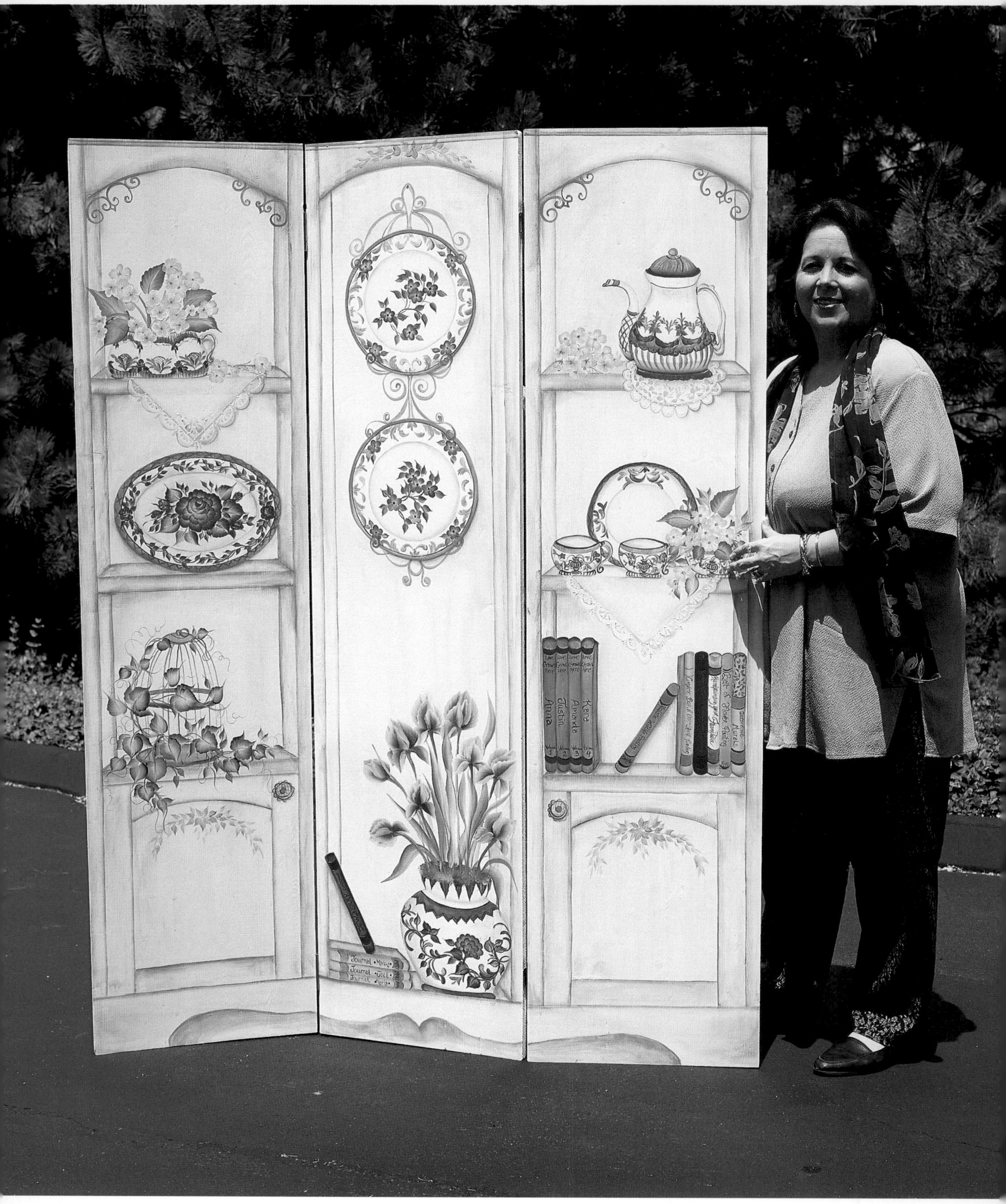

Anna
Justin
Amanda
Kara

Introduction

The concept of this book was created from many of the ideas that resulted from my interior decorating days. Sometimes a client of mine would have an unusual or sentimental piece she wanted to use as part of a room's decor, but the piece just wasn't right. So my thought was always... just paint it to fit! Decorative painting allows that alternative.

This book is for all those times when I had to stretch my abilities and to acknowledge that the only way to grow is to leave my comfort zone. With that in mind, I hope you will try some of these projects and in the process may discover a new depth to your own creativity.

I would like to tell you a true story that will help illustrate this point. My husband built custom homes for many years and worked with many interior decorators. One of the main things he learned was that often a homeowner wanted something a certain way but was unable to clearly explain what he or she wanted. And even though the interior decorator was a professional, many times she was not completely in tune with the owner's wishes.

So when I began decorating homes, my husband encouraged me to be a good listener. That turned out to be good advice, because many times I discovered that the client was not who I had perceived them to be.

There was one instance where I was finishing up an entire decorating project and applying the final touches and hanging pictures. Suddenly my well-travelled (and to this point, accommodating) client pulled out a couple of small tables she had acquired in her travels. Now, these tables would have been okay in a den (or better yet, in a dentist's office) but they would have been completely out of place in her elegant living room. She was determined to have me fit them in, and if it weren't for my husband's advice, I would have refused.

My client began to relate how she had acquired these pieces and the memories they brought for her. I realized that if I did not incorporate them into the room, she would upon my departure.

I was then able to see these pieces from her point of view and realized that with a little paint and a few new pieces of hardware, they would actually make a nice addition to her living room.

My client was delighted! What could have been a disaster turned out to be just the opposite.

Isn't decorative painting wonderful? Just think — a few brushstrokes and a little color can change an ordinary or unworkable piece of furniture into a family heirloom, a treasured addition to your home's decor, and an expression of your own creativity.

Materials

Paints and Mediums

For all the projects in this book, I used FolkArt acrylic paints made by Plaid. They come in small plastic squeeze bottles that are really handy to use, and can be found at any craft or art supply store. I like FolkArt paints not only because they're rich and creamy and easy to blend, but also because they're lightfast and permanent — so important when painting furniture. Because they're acrylic and water-based, clean-up is easy. And they come in so many different colors that you'll rarely have to mix your own.

Some of the colors used in these projects are called FolkArt Artists' Pigment. They're still bottled acrylic paints but they have more pigment in them so the colors are a little more saturated.

Each project in this book includes a color swatch chart of all the colors I used to paint each piece of furniture, so you shouldn't have any trouble matching colors if you prefer to use a different brand of acrylic paint.

I also use FolkArt's Floating Medium for subtle shading and to make some of my colors a little more transparent. I just mix the gel-like Floating Medium with my paint color on the palette, or I load my brush first with Floating Medium, then side load into my paint color.

On a few of the furniture pieces in this book I used a tiny amount of FolkArt's Gold Reflecting Medium. It comes in the same kind of handy squeeze bottle as the regular acrylic colors, but if you can't find it at your local store, try using FolkArt's Inca Gold Metallic instead.

Finally, to preserve and protect all your handpainted pieces of furniture, I recommend using Waterbase Varnish by FolkArt in the satin finish. After you have completed painting each piece, check it over to make sure you're happy with it. Let the paint dry completely, then apply at least two coats of the varnish, sanding between each coat. If you plan to use the piece outdoors, use a varnish that is formulated for exterior use.

Brushes

The brushes used in all my projects are the FolkArt One-Stroke brushes from Plaid. These can be purchased at any arts and crafts supply store and they come in the sizes I use most often: a ¾-inch (19mm) flat, a no. 12 flat, no. 6 flat, no. 2 flat, a no. 2 script liner, a no. 1 script liner, a large and small scruffy brush, and a fan brush. The bristles on all these brushes are synthetic (except for the natural-bristle scruffy brushes) and were designed especially for my painting technique.

Supplies

Most of the other supplies used for these projects can be found around the house or at art supply stores and home improvement centers. I don't use a fancy artist's palette for my paints — I just use plain white Styrofoam plates. The paint doesn't absorb into the plates; they're lightweight and easy to hold; and when you're finished, just throw them away!

I always keep a paper towel next to my painting area for blotting excess water out of my brush and for general cleanups. Clear plastic wrap can be used to make interesting "faux finish" effects. And a rectangular household sponge can be used to paint shading (see Project 10 for step-by-step photos on painting a trompe l'oeil cabinet with a household sponge).

I use sandpaper and sanding blocks to smooth out my raw wood furniture pieces, then foam brushes or rollers for basecoating them, sanding lightly between coats.

A square plastic brush basin is very handy for cleaning paint out of your brushes. It has two separate compartments for dirty water and clean water.

Finally, I use tracing paper, black or gray graphite paper and a stylus or pencil to transfer my patterns onto my project pieces. These items can be found at art supply stores.

How to Load Your Brushes with Paint

Side Loading

1 First, dampen your brush in clean water, then blot excess off on a paper towel. Work your dampened brush back and forth into the clear, gel-like Floating Medium.

2 To side load your brush, stroke the prepared brush into your desired color, stroking next to the puddle of paint, not into its middle. Work the brush back and forth to load paint into both sides of the brush.

Double Loading

1 To double load your brush, dampen it in clean water, blot, then dip one corner into your first color.

2 Flip your brush over and dip into the second color. Don't be concerned if your bristles split — they'll come back together as you work the paint in.

3 On your palette, use a lot of pressure to work paint into the bristles.

4 Reverse direction and stroke a second time going the opposite way. Keep the white side of the brush on the same side all the time.

5 Repeat steps 3 and 4, working your brush back and forth, picking up more paint on the corners two or three times. The brush is fully loaded when the paint comes at least two-thirds of the way up the bristles.

6 Now that the brush is fully loaded, very gently dip a corner into each color. You need to pick up more paint for almost every stroke. Don't stroke on your palette anymore after you've dipped the corners. Just begin painting on your surface.

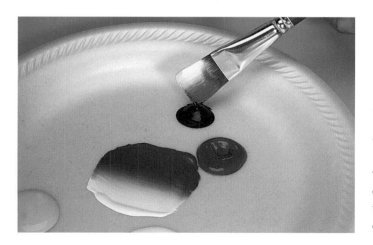

Multi-Loading

7 To add more than two colors to your brush, dip the already-dipped corners into two other colors, ending up with two colors on each corner. I usually dip the darker corner into the darkest color, and the lighter corner into the lightest color. Do not work these third and fourth colors into your brush. Just leave them on the corners.

Loading the Script Liner

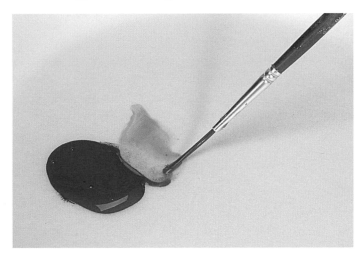 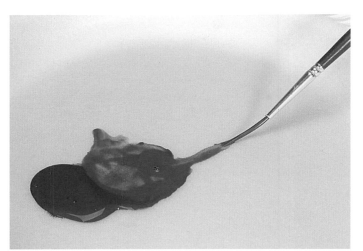

1 The script liner is the only brush I use where I may add water to the paint. Dip the bristles into water and make circular motions next to your puddle of paint on the palette, picking up a little bit of paint and working it into the water.

2 When the puddle has an inky consistency, roll the bristles as you pull out of the puddle so paint doesn't drip off your brush.

How to Use Floating Medium

1 I like to use a "gel" floating medium when I'm getting very dry strokes because the paint is soaking into the wood, or because the climate is very dry. Fully load your brush with the desired paint colors, then dip the chisel edge of the brush into the floating medium.

If floating medium is not available, you can use water. Dip just the chisel edge into water, but be careful not to overdo it.

2 Work the floating medium into the bristles back and forth on the palette. But be careful — your colors may become muddy if you pick up floating medium too often. ("Muddy" means you don't see your shading and highlighting colors — you get an overblended look.) I usually pick up more floating medium every third or fourth stroke when I'm painting.

Loading the Scruffy Brush

A "scruffy" brush can be a one-inch (25mm) flat brush that may be worn out. Just cut the bristles off to leave a flat, stubby surface, then fluff them out with your finger to the desired shape.

My scruffy is oval shaped with soft, natural bristles, which makes it possible to pounce the bristles and have them spring back. I like to use this brush for moss, grass, and flower centers.

1 With a dry scruffy, pounce with pressure into a puddle of your first color. Be sure to pounce into the edge of the paint puddle, not the center.

2 Repeat this step with the other half of the brush into your second color. Pounce firmly into the paint.

3 This is how your scruffy brush should look when it's correctly and fully loaded.

4 You can multi-load your scruffy just as you can any other brush. Pounce your loaded scruffy on the palette, then pounce again into additional colors, darker colors to the darker side of the brush, lighter colors to the light side.

Basic Painting Techniques

Painting Vines

1 To paint vines, use the chisel edge of your flat brush. If your brush is double loaded, always lead with the lighter color. Slightly tilt the lighter corner up. This drags the green (or darker) bristles behind, automatically shading your vine and highlighting it at the same time.

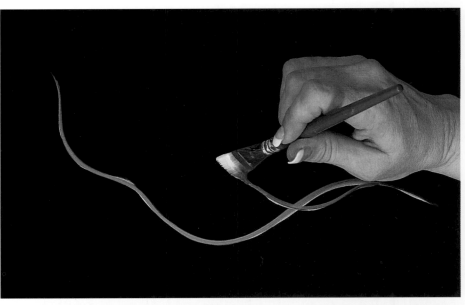

2 To make the vines flow naturally, you need to move your whole arm, not just the brush. When your vines are finished, begin placing a leaf by touching the chisel edge of the brush in a V-shape, keeping the green side toward the ends of the V. The next photo shows how this leaf was completed, then connected to the vine via a stem.

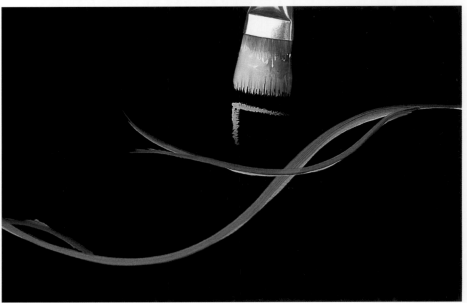

Painting Leaves

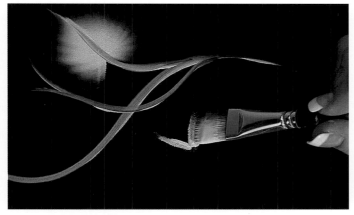

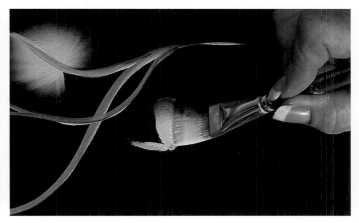

1 Never start a leaf right on top of the vine. Leaves connect to a vine via stems, so start your leaf away from the vine. Again, mark your starting points with a "V" touched on with the chisel edge of your double-loaded flat brush.

2 For the first half of the leaf, start your brush on one line of the V, holding the green to the outer edge of the leaf.

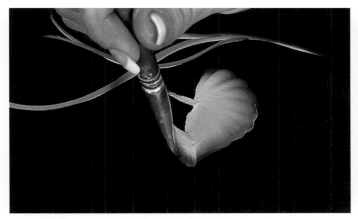

3 Wiggle your brush as you stroke, watching the green edge to get the desired shape. Pull the green all the way to the tip of the leaf, then lift up onto the chisel edge to finish. If you want a smooth-edged leaf, don't wiggle the brush, just stroke it smoothly.

4 Paint the other half of the leaf, starting on the V and keeping the green of your brush to the outer edge of the leaf.

5 With the chisel edge of your flat brush, pull a stem from the vine halfway into the leaf while the leaf is still wet. Lead with the lighter color and stay up on the tip of the chisel edge so the stem doesn't get too heavy.

Painting a One-Stroke Leaf

1 Double load your flat brush with green and either yellow or white. With the green side of the brush to the outer edge of the leaf, push down on the bristles so they're bent almost to the ferrule and begin your stroke.

2 As you continue the stroke, turn the green corner of the brush toward where you want the tip of the leaf to end.

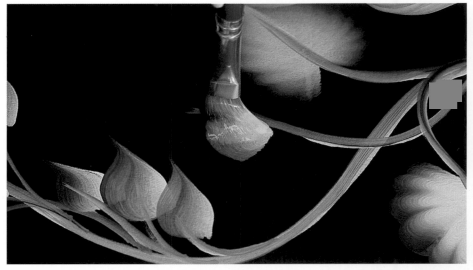

3 Lift the brush as you slide to the point, ending up on the chisel edge of your brush. Now pull a stem into the leaf from the vine, leading with the lighter color.

Creating a Natural Growth Pattern

1 As you paint your leaves and vines, check that they have a natural looking growth pattern to them. In this example, you can see that I've painted the leaves going all in one direction — not a natural look.

2 Use your fingers to indicate the direction the leaves are pointing.

3 Now turn your hand so your fingers are pointing the other direction. Now you can see that you'll need to add some leaves on the other side of the vine.

4 Doesn't this look more natural? All I did was add a few more one-stroke leaves to the left side of the vine.

Curlicues and Calyxes

1 Curlicues, or tendrils of new growth, are easy to paint with a script liner loaded with inky paint (see page 14, "Loading the Script Liner"). Holding the brush handle perpendicular to the surface, brace your pinky finger against the surface and move your whole arm in a smooth flowing motion.

2 To paint a calyx (the protective leaves that grow up over a flower bud), double load a small flat brush with green and a lighter color such as yellow. Touch the chisel edge at the base of the bud, leaning the lighter corner of the brush toward the top of the bud. Stroke upward around the bud, lifting up to the chisel edge. Repeat on the other side of the bud.

3 The center calyx is painted the same way, but the stroke is shorter — go only halfway up the bud.

4 Pull a stem from beneath the bud and slide back to your main vine to connect.

Painting Fern Leaves

1 Double load a small flat brush, and paint the stem in the center. Pull fern leaves toward the stem by starting up on the chisel edge of the brush, then pushing down on the bristles.

2 To taper each leaflet toward the stem end, lift back up to the chisel edge as you get closer to the stem. For natural looking ferns, overlap some of the leaflets.

Transferring the Pattern

Patterns for all of the projects in this book are provided for you. The easiest way to transfer a pattern to your chosen surface is to first enlarge the pattern to the percentage given (any photocopy center can do this for you). Then place a piece of tracing paper over the enlarged pattern. Trace the pattern with a pen.

Now position the tracing paper on your surface and tape it down in a few places with low-tack tape. Slide some graphite paper in between the tracing paper and the surface, making sure the graphite side is toward the surface.

Using a stylus or pencil, trace only the outer edges of the design's major elements, not all the little details. Check your work by lifting up a corner every once in a while to make sure you haven't missed a line. Remove the graphite and the tracing paper, and you're ready to paint!

Child's Tall Chest

MATERIALS

PAINT: FolkArt by Plaid **(AP) = FolkArt Artists' Pigment**

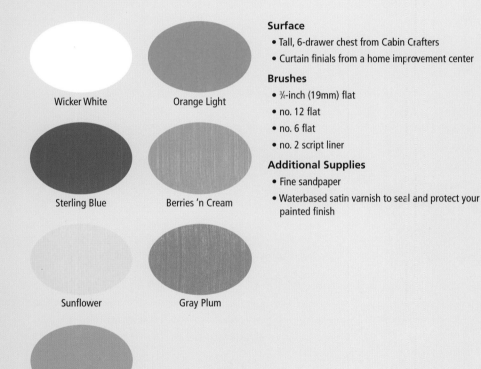

Wicker White

Orange Light

Sterling Blue

Berries 'n Cream

Sunflower

Gray Plum

Basil Green

Surface
- Tall, 6-drawer chest from Cabin Crafters
- Curtain finials from a home improvement center

Brushes
- ¾-inch (19mm) flat
- no. 12 flat
- no. 6 flat
- no. 2 script liner

Additional Supplies
- Fine sandpaper
- Waterbased satin varnish to seal and protect your painted finish

This tall, six-drawer chest is perfect for a child's little treasures. It started out as a plain, unfinished wood cabinet. I bought two wooden curtain finials, screwed and glued the finials to the top, and painted the whole thing with two to three basecoats of Wicker White, sanding lightly between coats. The designs painted on the drawer fronts and finials are so whimsical and easy to do you won't need a pattern. Just paint them freehand!

Paint Colorful Designs

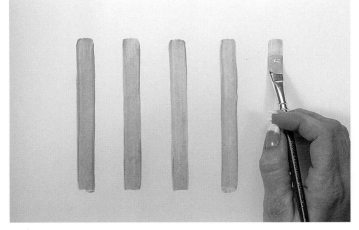

1 Fully load a no. 12 flat brush with Berries 'n Cream. Starting at the top edge of the first drawer front, stroke downward to make pink stripes.

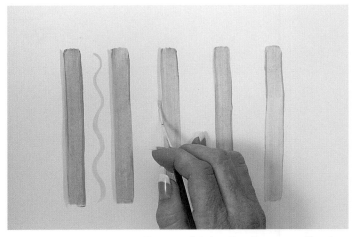

2 Using a no. 2 script liner and inky Sunflower, pull yellow pinstripes down the side of the pink stripes. Then pull a wavy yellow stripe down the center.

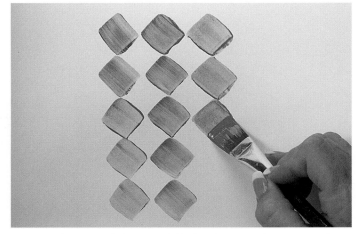

3 For the second drawer, fully load a ¾-inch (19mm) flat with Sterling Blue. Paint columns of angled checks from top to bottom, with each check touching the corner of the previous check.

4 For the third drawer, fully load a ¾-inch (19mm) flat with Sunflower. Paint wavy yellow strokes from left to right. Using a no. 2 script liner loaded with inky Sterling Blue, add pinstripes between the yellow waves.

5 For the fourth drawer, load a ¾-inch (19mm) flat with Gray Plum and paint diagonal stripes. Add wavy lines of inky Sunflower using a no. 2 script liner.

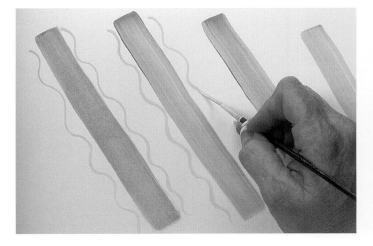

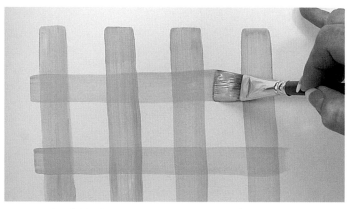

6 On the fifth drawer, paint a plaid with Basil Green on a ¾-inch (19mm) flat. Pull vertical strokes from top to bottom, then horizontals from left to right.

7 On the bottom drawer, paint circles of different sizes with a no. 12 flat fully loaded with Orange Light.

8 With inky Basil Green on a no. 2 script liner, paint a fine outline around each orange circle.

9 The decorative finials for the top of the chest had already been basecoated with Wicker White. Then I loaded Berries 'n Cream on a no. 6 flat and painted pink spiral stripes around the base, then a ring of Basil Green. I added Sunflower on the bigger ball, Basil Green vertical stripes, and finally Sterling Blue on the top ball. It's easier to paint the finials first, then attach them to the chest when the paint is completely dry.

10 The side panels of the chest were freehanded with a diagonal design. I loaded a no. 12 flat with Sterling Blue and pulled diagonal striping from top to bottom. I repeated this, reversing the diagonals. I added dots of Wicker White in the middle of all the criss-crosses. With Sunflower, I painted a tear-drop in the center of each square by pushing down on the chisel edge of the flat brush and stroking upward.

Cherries & Berries Desk Top

MATERIALS

PAINT: FolkArt by Plaid   **(AP) = FolkArt Artists' Pigment**

Bayberry

Engine Red

Burnt Carmine (AP)

Wicker White

Midnight

Thicket

Burnt Umber (AP)

Yellow Ochre (AP)

Sunflower

Butter Pecan

Surface
- Wooden desk top and metal stand by Robinson's Woods

Brushes
- ¾-inch (19mm) flat
- no. 12 flat
- no. 10 flat
- no. 6 flat
- no. 2 script liner

Additional Supplies
- Floating Medium
- Fine sandpaper
- Waterbased satin varnish

The tilted desk top by itself would be a treasure, but add the metal stand and it becomes a charming accessory to a kitchen or family room. I basecoated the wooden desk top and the lower shelf with Bayberry, sanding lightly between coats. When the final basecoat was completely dry, I transferred the pattern for the cherries and berries design. For the metal stand I used red spray paint to accentuate the red cherries.

Branches, Vines and Leaves

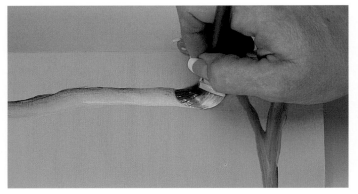

1 Basecoat all sides of the desktop with Bayberry. Double load a ¾-inch (19mm) flat brush with Burnt Umber and Wicker White. Paint the larger branches around the perimeter, leading with the white edge of the brush.

2 With the same brush, add smaller cherry branches to the lower right corner and top middle.

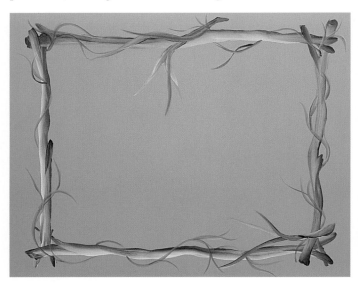

3 Double load a no. 12 flat brush with Sunflower and Thicket and paint wandering vines up and around the branches, staying up on the chisel edge of the brush.

4 Now double load a no. 10 flat brush with Thicket and Sunflower, and paint the larger two-sided leaves. Then add one-stroke leaves with the same colors on a no. 6 flat.

5 Add clusters of cherry leaves onto the two cherry branches with Butter Pecan and Thicket double loaded on a no. 10 flat brush.

Rosebuds and Berries

6 Double load a no. 6 flat with Engine Red and Wicker White. Paint the upper petal of the rosebud using a C-stroke. Remember to keep the Wicker White side of the brush toward the top.

7 For the lower petal, start and end the same as the upper petal, but paint a U-stroke, keeping the Wicker White toward the top.

8 To layer the rosebud, add a third petal on top of, but a little lower than, the second petal.

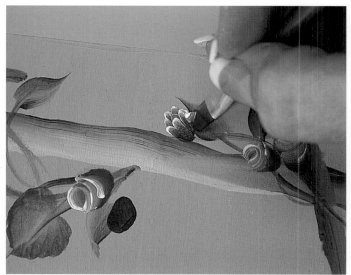

9 After all the rosebuds are finished, load Midnight on a no. 6 flat and basecoat the berry shapes.

10 With Midnight on the same no. 6 flat brush, side load into Wicker White on one corner of the brush and make tiny little C-strokes for the seeds.

Cherries and White Flowers

11 To paint the cherries, load a no. 6 flat with Engine Red and side load into Burnt Carmine. Paint each cherry with the Burnt Carmine to the outer edge to give a rounded look.

12 Painting cherries is easy! Just paint half of the cherry, then flip your brush over to paint the other half, always keeping the Burnt Carmine to the outer edge.

13 Load your no. 6 flat with Floating Medium, stroke into Wicker White on your palette, and paint highlights on the cherries.

14 To paint the white blossoms, double load a no. 6 flat with Yellow Ochre and Wicker White. Form a five-petal flower with rippled edges, holding Wicker White to each petal's outer edge.

Pattern for Cherries & Berries Desk Top

This pattern may be hand-traced or photocopied for personal use only. Enlarge at 213% to bring it up to full size.

15 For the finishing details, double load a no. 2 script liner with Thicket and Sunflower. Use the tip of bristles to dot the centers of the white blossoms. Using the same brush, touch the top of each cherry and pull back to the branch for stems.

Add calyxes to the rosebuds and the berries using a no. 6 flat double loaded with Sunflower and Thicket. Load a no. 2 script liner with inky Thicket to make curlicues for the new vines.

Finally, check your work and add more rosebuds, berries or leaves if needed, continuing the design onto the flat area of the desktop.

On the drawer fronts, I added mini versions of the cherries and white blossoms (see page 26), and I painted the metal stand red to accentuate the cherries.

3-Drawer Chest with Florals

MATERIALS

PAINT: FolkArt by Plaid   **AP = FolkArt Artists' Pigment**

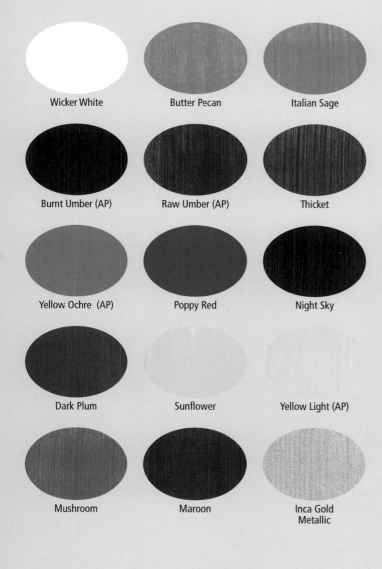

Wicker White

Butter Pecan

Italian Sage

Burnt Umber (AP)

Raw Umber (AP)

Thicket

Yellow Ochre (AP)

Poppy Red

Night Sky

Dark Plum

Sunflower

Yellow Light (AP)

Mushroom

Maroon

Inca Gold Metallic

Surface
- Wooden 3-drawer chest on cast iron stand from Robinson's Woods

Brushes
- ¾-inch (19mm) flat
- no. 12 flat
- no. 8 flat
- no. 6 flat
- no. 2 script liner
- small scruffy

Additional Supplies
- FolkArt Floating Medium
- Fine sandpaper
- Sponge roller
- Clear plastic wrap
- Tracing paper
- Stylus
- Gray graphite
- Gold Reflecting Medium (opt.)
- Waterbased satin varnish

This chest reminds me a little bit of some old pieces I have seen around that aren't too pretty anymore and need to be given new life. The chest in the picture is actually a new, unfinished wood piece I bought that came with its own metal stand. I replaced the knobs that were on the drawers with clear glass knobs from a home improvement center. And the subtle "faux finish," which was actually applied after the basecoat but before the floral designs, can help hide any slight dents or scratches in the wood.

Patterns For Flowers on 3-Drawer Chest

The large pattern is for the top of the chest; the smaller one in the center is for the drawer fronts. These patterns may be hand-traced or photocopied for personal use only. Enlarge at 385% to bring them up to full size.

Paint an Easy "Faux Finish"

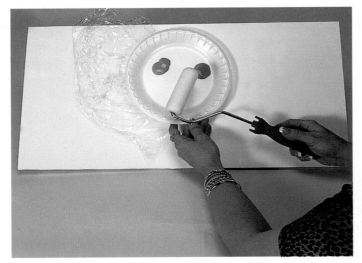

1 First sand your surface to a smooth finish. Start with the top of the chest and basecoat with Wicker White, two to three coats, sanding between each coat. Put Butter Pecan and Italian Sage on your palette. Dampen your sponge roller in clean water, then roll into the two colors randomly but don't blend. Have a piece of clear plastic wrap ready.

2 Roll the two colors onto the surface, covering a small area at a time. Don't roll too much, you don't want your colors to blend.

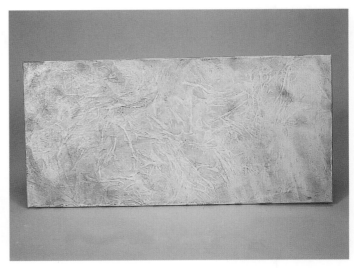

3 Lay a piece of clear plastic wrap down over the paint and pat it down. Don't smooth out the wrinkles. Lift, and if needed, lay back down to cover all areas painted. Pull off the wrap.

4 Here's how the "faux finish" looks — it's not too uniform. It has a random, aged look.

Paint Branches and Leaves

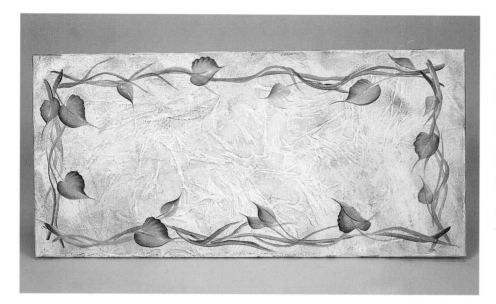

1 Load a ¾-inch (19mm) flat with Raw Umber and Wicker White. Then pick up Floating Medium if needed. Paint the branches around the perimeter using the chisel edge of the brush. Keep the branches loose and flowing. Fill in with additional branches. Take a ¾-inch (19mm) flat double loaded with Mushroom and Thicket and dip the Thicket corner into Raw Umber. Paint all the large leaves, then start adding smaller one-stroke leaves with a no. 12 flat and the same colors.

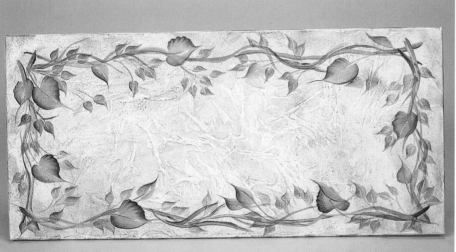

2 With the same no. 12 flat, pick up Floating Medium on your brush and fill in clusters of even smaller one-stroke leaves. Pull stems into the leaves with a no. 2 script liner.

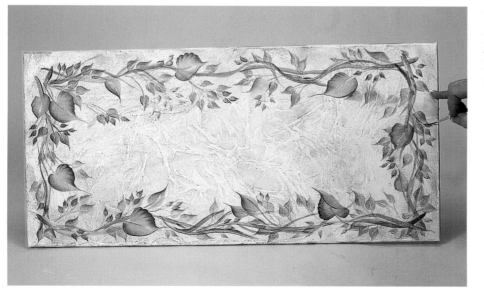

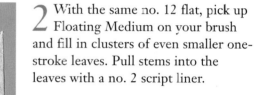

3 Paint very small shadow leaves with Mushroom and Floating Medium double loaded on a no. 6 flat. Pull stems into the shadow leaves with the same colors on a script liner.

Add Pink Flowers

1 Using a no. 12 flat double loaded with Maroon and Wicker White, push down, wiggle and lift the brush to paint each petal in a sea-shell shape. Keep the white on the outer edge, and paint five to six petals for each blossom.

2 Add a flower bud here and there, stroking a partial petal on the back of the bud.

3 Layer partial petals to build the bud, always keeping the white side of your brush toward the top edge.

4 Add a little green base to each bud with Thicket and Raw Umber on the chisel edge of your no. 12 flat. Make little strokes to attach the stems.

5 To paint the flower centers, load a no. 2 script liner with Burnt Umber then drag the bristles through a puddle of white paint. Dot the centers with the tip of the bristles.

Paint White Blossoms

1 The white blossoms are larger than the pink ones but they're painted with the same technique. Double load Mushroom and Wicker White on a no. 12 flat to paint the petals, again keeping the white side of the brush toward the outer edge of each petal.

2 Pounce centers in with a small scruffy brush loaded with Yellow Ochre.

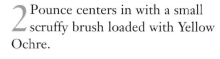

3 With the same scruffy brush, pounce into Thicket and Sunflower on your palette, then lightly pounce on top of the Yellow Ochre center.

Purple and Yellow Blossoms

1 To paint the purple blossoms, double load Dark Plum and Wicker White on a no. 12 flat. Start on the chisel edge, push down on the bristles and paint a tightly curved, teardrop-shaped petal with the white to the outside edge. Lift back up to the chisel edge to complete the petal. Stroke five or more petals for each blossom.

2 An easy way to paint nice round centers is to touch the end of your brush handle into Sunflower, then dot each blossom center with the tip of the handle.

1 To paint the yellow flowers, load Yellow Ochre and Wicker White on a no. 12 flat. Keep the Yellow Ochre toward the outer edge of the petals. Stroke the same as for the purple flowers, but leave more space between petals for a more open blossom.

2 With inky Burnt Umber on a no. 2 script liner, touch the center and pull little stamens outward.

3 With the same brush, stroke through Wicker White on your palette, then dot the ends of each stamen.

Trumpet Vine

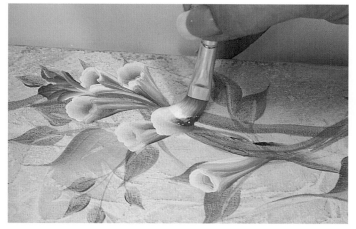

1 To add variety to the flower shapes, paint some pink trumpet flowers with Poppy Red and Wicker White double loaded on a no. 12 flat. Wiggle the white edge of the brush upward to shape the back part of the opening.

2 To shape the front of the opening, use the same brush and start a little lower over the back part. Wiggle the brush, with the white edge toward the top.

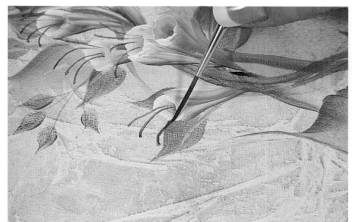

3 Now pull the brush straight down on its chisel edge to fill in the rest of the front petal.

4 Paint three or four long curving stamens on each blossom with inky Thicket on a no. 2 script liner. Start at the top of the stamen and pull back toward the opening.

5 Dot the tip of each stamen with Wicker White and Yellow Ochre on your script liner.

Blue Flowers

1 These five-petal blue flowers are painted with a combination of Night Sky and Wicker White on a no. 12 flat. Keeping Night Sky to the outer edge, stroke upward to the point, then pull back down on the other side. Add a couple of buds in different stages of opening, using the same stroke.

2 Dot in centers with a no. 2 script liner double loaded with Yellow Light and Wicker White.

3 Here's how the top of the chest looks with all the blossoms and leaves finished. I added some curlicues of new stem growth with inky Thicket on a no. 2 script liner.

Little Butterflies

1 Double load a no. 12 flat with Wicker White and Yellow Ochre. Start on the chisel edge, push down on the bristles and lift back up to form the large back wing.

2 Pick up more paint and use the same stroke to overlap the back wing with the front wing.

3 Leading with Wicker White on the chisel edge, paint the bottom back wing, then overlap with the bottom front wing.

4 With inky Burnt Umber on a no. 2 script liner, touch with the tip of the brush to form the head. Then lift up and pull away to form the body.

5 For the butterfly's antennas, use the same brush with inky Burnt Umber and make light, curving strokes.

6 If you wish, you can outline each wing with the same brush and inky Burnt Umber.

Bumblebee

1 The body of the bumblebee is painted with Yellow Ochre on a no. 6 flat. Dot the head on with Burnt Umber. Then load a no. 8 flat with Wicker White and stroke on back and front wings, the same as the butterfly.

2 With a no. 1 script liner and inky Burnt Umber, make little parallel strokes to form furry stripes on the body.

3 Use a no. 2 script liner and inky Burnt Umber to outline and stroke veins on the wings. Let dry. Soften the wing color with a bit of Inca Gold Metallic (or Gold Reflecting Medium).

4 For the antennas and legs, use inky Burnt Umber on a no. 2 script liner. Keep a light touch to achieve these very fine lines.

A Dragonfly and a Moth

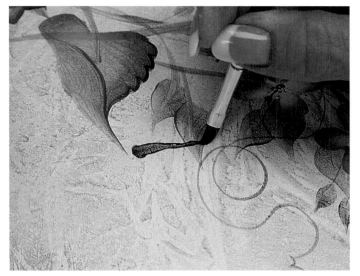

1 Load a no. 6 flat with Raw Umber and a little Thicket and paint the body of the dragonfly. Start with your brush flat for the widest part, then turn and lift up to the chisel edge for the narrower tail.

2 Stroke on long, oval wings with a no. 8 flat fully loaded with Wicker White, then side loaded into Raw Umber. Keep the Raw Umber on the outer edges. Let dry.

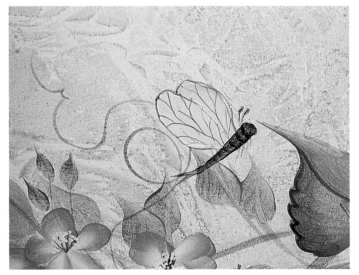

3 Add details to the dragonfly, like antennas, wing veins and stripes on the body, using the same colors and techniques as for the bumblebee.

4 To paint a little moth, use the same colors as for the dragonfly. Paint the moth's body first, then add wings and antennas.

Finished Top of Chest

Here's how the top of the chest looks with all the flowers in place and the little insects buzzing around. I think adding the little critters gives this floral design the feel of a real garden in the height of summer.

Completed Drawer Fronts

The three drawer fronts are painted with the same floral
elements as the top of the chest. Just adapt them to fit
the size and shape of your chest of drawers. After all
painting is finished, seal the entire chest with two to
three coats of waterbased satin varnish. I added clear
crystal drawer pulls for a touch of elegance.

Flowers and Birds on 2-Door Cabinet

MATERIALS

PAINT: FolkArt by Plaid   **(AP) = FolkArt Artists' Pigment**

Licorice

Raw Umber (AP)

Burnt Umber (AP)

Wicker White

Thicket

Butter Pecan

Sunflower

Periwinkle

Rose Shimmer Metallic

Yellow Light (AP)

Night Sky

Yellow Ochre (AP)

Burnt Carmine (AP)

Poppy Red

School Bus Yellow

Surface
- 2-door cabinet from Robinson's Woods

Brushes
- ¾-inch (19mm) flat
- no. 12 flat
- no. 10 flat
- no. 6 flat
- nos. 1 and 2 script liners
- large and small scruffy brushes

Additional Supplies
- Floating Medium
- Fine sandpaper
- White graphite paper
- Stylus or pencil
- 4 wooden curtain finials for the cabinet's feet (optional)

Any type of old or new two-door storage cabinet you may have would work for this design. I love the way the black background dramatizes the bright colors of the birds and flowers. The cabinet's feet are actually wooden curtain finials I found at a home store and painted black. They add a touch of sophistication and flair, and give the cabinet a lighter look.

Pattern for Left Door

These patterns may be hand-traced or photocopied for personal use only. Enlarge at 263% to bring them up to full size.

Pattern for Right Door

Bird's Nest and Vines

1 Basecoat the entire cabinet with Licorice. Let it dry, then transfer the patterns onto the two door fronts. To paint the bird's nest, base on a white area for the inside of the nest. With a no. 12 flat double loaded with Wicker White and Burnt Umber, use the chisel edge of the brush to paint little twigs around and around to form the nest. Paint the hanging vines with the same chisel-edge strokes.

2 Using a ¾-inch (19mm) flat double loaded with Sunflower and Thicket, paint the vines around the nest, stroking upward from the bottom. Paint the vines on the hanging feeder stroking down from the top.

3 With the same brush and colors, add Floating Medium and paint in the grasses and stems with upward strokes of the brush. Be sure to stay up on the chisel edge and move your whole arm to achieve an airy, natural look.

4 Pounce in moss on the feeder (avoiding the bird) with a large scruffy brush multi-loaded with Raw Umber, Thicket and Wicker White.

Leaves and Details

5 Paint the daisy leaves with Thicket, a lot of Floating Medium and a little Sunflower, with the Sunflower toward the outer edges because of the dark background.

6 Fill in the rest of the leaves on both vines with Thicket, Yellow Light and Floating Medium.

7 Paint corn kernels in the feeder with Sunflower and Yellow Ochre pounced on with a scruffy. Then go back in with a no. 6 flat and Sunflower and make individual kernels, occasionally picking up a little Burnt Umber on your brush for variety. To paint the eggs in the nest, load a no. 12 flat with Night Sky and Wicker White and paint the egg in the back first, then the two in front. Keep the Night Sky toward the outer edge. To create the fuzzy inside of the nest, pounce a small scruffy loaded with Burnt Umber, Raw Umber and Wicker White.

Paint the Bluebird

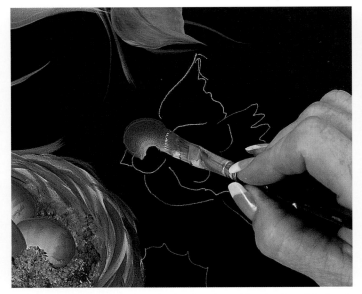

8 Begin the bluebird with the head and back. Double load a no. 12 flat with Periwinkle and Night Sky. Paint the head with Night Sky to the outer edge.

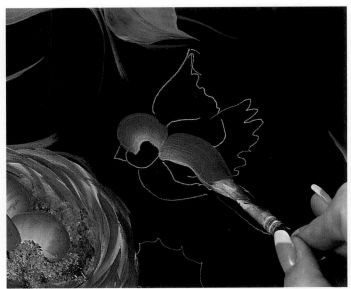

9 Stroke down the bluebird's back with the flat of the brush, ending up on the chisel edge.

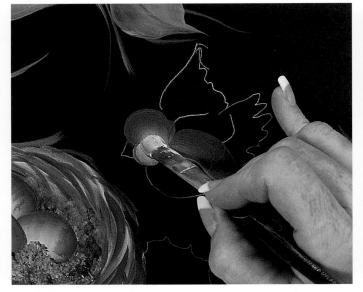

10 Pick up Wicker White on the same brush and paint the bluebird's cheeks.

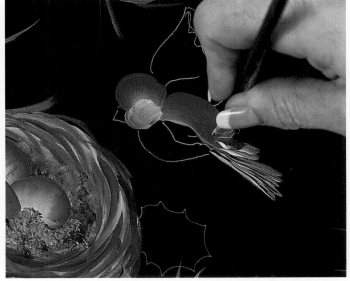

11 The tail feathers are painted with Night Sky and Wicker White. Pull from the longest tail feather back toward the body, staying up on the chisel edge of the brush.

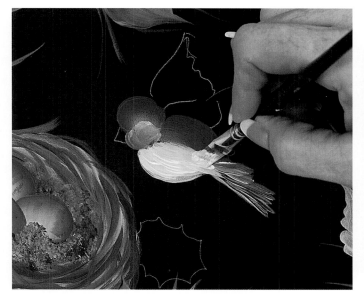

12 Paint the breast with Yellow Light and Wicker White shaping it with the flat of the brush. Go back in on the chisel edge and detail some soft feathers on the breast.

13 Double load Wicker White and Night Sky on your flat brush and paint the back wing.

14 With the same brush and colors, add the longest feathers along the back wing, pulling the Night Sky from the outer edge in toward the wing.

15 Double load Periwinkle and White on the same brush and add a second layer of feathers. Be sure to stay up on the chisel edge to get those fine, feathery lines.

16 To paint the front wing, load your flat brush with Night Sky, Periwinkle and Wicker White and pull a long smooth stroke, overlapping the back wing.

17 Add a layer of outer feathers with Periwinkle and Wicker White on the same brush, pulling the Periwinkle toward the wing's outer edge.

18 Now pick up Yellow Light and Wicker White on the same brush for the second layer of feathers.

19 Finish the front wing with a couple more layers of Periwinkle and Wicker White.

20 Load a no. 1 script liner with Burnt Umber and add a neck band, eye and beak with short strokes.

21 Dot in an eye with Licorice, and add white highlights on the eye and beak.

22 Paint the other two bluebirds the same way using the same colors. Remember to paint the feathers underneath first. Start with the tail feathers, then the left wing, then the right.

Daisies and Morning Glories

23 Paint yellow daisies with School Bus Yellow, Yellow Ochre and Wicker White on a no. 10 flat. Pull the petals toward the daisy centers on the open flowers. For the buds, pull the petals toward the stems.

Wipe out excess yellow on your brush and pick up Wicker White. Repeat the same strokes for the white daisies. Pounce in the centers with Burnt Umber and Sunflower on a small scruffy brush.

24 To paint the pink morning glories, double load Rose Shimmer and Wicker White on a no. 12 flat. Keeping the Rose Shimmer to the outside edge, begin painting the scallop shape of the trumpet, creating little "points" with your brush as you go.

25 Complete the entire trumpet, wiggling your brush to make the scalloped edge and keeping the Rose Shimmer to the outside.

26 Use the chisel edge of the same brush to add streaks to the throat of the flower from the center outward.

27 With the same double-loaded brush, start at each point of the flower and pull the white corner of the brush from each point back to the throat to make ribs.

28 Load a no. 1 script liner with School Bus Yellow and Thicket. Pull downward strokes to paint the center of throat.

29 Finish up the front of the cabinet with little bumblebees and a butterfly or two. The bumblebees' bodies are Yellow Ochre and Burnt Umber; their wings are Wicker White. The butterfly's wings are Periwinkle and Wicker White, and the body is Licorice. See pages 43-45 for painting instructions for the insects.

Dogwood Blossoms

30 On the top of the cabinet I painted a branch of pink dogwood blossoms. Double load a no. 12 flat with Poppy Red and Wicker White. Holding white to the outer edge, stroke four large petals with a small indentation at the center of the curve.

31 With a small scruffy brush double loaded with Yellow Ochre and Burnt Carmine, pounce on the dogwood centers.

32 Load a no. 2 script liner with inky Burnt Carmine. Pull veins from the center out on each petal.

33 Load a no. 6 flat with Floating Medium, then side load Burnt Carmine and shade the little indentations on the four petals.

Wildflowers on Side Panel

34 To dress up the side panels of the cabinet, you could add any sort of wildflower you like. I painted a sedum because I like the lacy look of the blossoms. With a ¾-inch (19mm) flat double loaded with Sunflower and Thicket plus Floating Medium, pull short stemlets and large leaves, holding the yellow to the outer edge of the leaves.

35 Using a large scruffy brush double loaded with Yellow Ochre and Wicker White, pounce on the arch shaped blossom of the sedum, keeping it light and airy. Highlight where the stem touches the stemlets with a little bit of yellow.

When you have completed the cabinet, protect the painting with a few coats of waterbased satin varnish. If you wish, paint four wooden curtain finials black and screw them to the bottom four corners of the cabinet to serve as ball feet.

Sea Shell Trunk

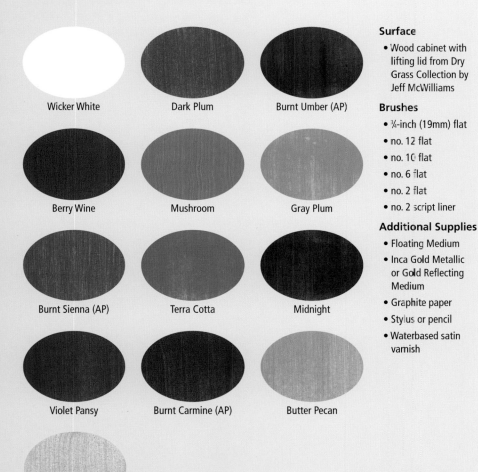

MATERIALS

PAINT: FolkArt by Plaid   **(AP) = FolkArt Artists' Pigment**

Wicker White

Dark Plum

Burnt Umber (AP)

Berry Wine

Mushroom

Gray Plum

Burnt Sienna (AP)

Terra Cotta

Midnight

Violet Pansy

Burnt Carmine (AP)

Butter Pecan

Inca Gold Metallic

Surface
• Wood cabinet with lifting lid from Dry Grass Collection by Jeff McWilliams

Brushes
• ¾-inch (19mm) flat
• no. 12 flat
• no. 10 flat
• no. 6 flat
• no. 2 flat
• no. 2 script liner

Additional Supplies
• Floating Medium
• Inca Gold Metallic or Gold Reflecting Medium
• Graphite paper
• Stylus or pencil
• Waterbased satin varnish

This spacious flat-lidded trunk is a great place to store your family's beach vacation photos, souvenirs and scrapbooks. The sea shell and rope motif would work on any size hope chest, blanket chest or other storage piece, and would look especially nice in a vacation or seaside cottage. I basecoated the entire trunk and lid with Wicker White, sanding lightly between coats. The legs are accented with Mushroom and Inca Gold Metallic.

Rope and Shell Trim on Lid

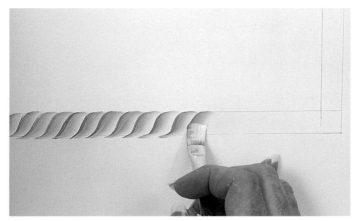

1 Use a ruler to measure a half-inch (1.3cm) band and pencil in all around the perimeter of the lid for the rope. With Mushroom and Wicker White double loaded on a no. 12 flat, start on the top pencil line and make a series of S-strokes coming down to the bottom pencil line.

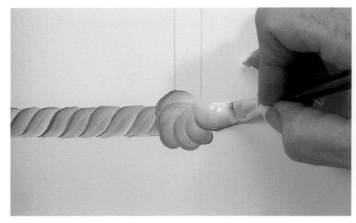

2 To make the corner knot, paint C-strokes to form almost a full circle.

3 For the other end of the knot, start on the perpendicular part of the rope and stroke in toward the center of the knot.

4 Finish the rest of the rope and the knots at the other three corners. Let dry. Trace on the rest of the design.

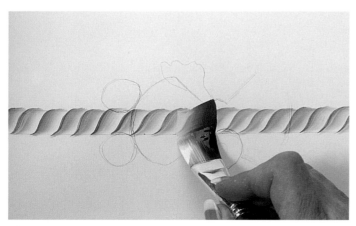

5 To paint the shell, load a ¾-inch (19mm) flat with Burnt Carmine and Wicker White. Paint the base first, holding Burnt Carmine to the outer edge.

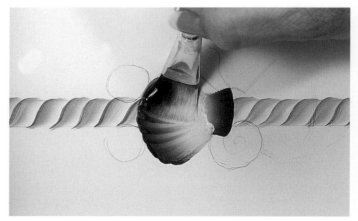

6 Paint a curving wiggle edge from one side to the other to form the clam shell.

7 Dip the corner of the same brush in Burnt Carmine and stroke over the base to give it a curve.

8 Blend that curved stroke into the shell with the chisel edge of your brush, leading with the white edge.

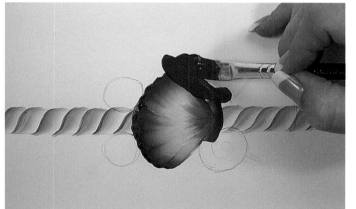

9 Double load Violet Pansy and Midnight on a no. 12 flat to make the small, dark shells on either side of the clam shell. Make sure to hold Midnight to the outer edge.

10 Paint a second layer, then a third layer on the small side shell, using the same brush.

11 With Burnt Umber and Wicker White double loaded on a no. 10 flat, paint the snail shell by spiralling inward from the outside edge, keeping the Burnt Umber to the outer edge as you go.

12 Double load a no. 2 flat with Burnt Umber and Floating Medium. Paint tiger stripes on the spiral shell from the outer edge toward the center. Add Violet Pansy and Midnight to the same brush and paint a little circle in the middle of the shell.

13 With Mushroom and Wicker White on a no. 6 flat, paint the little snail shells the same way as the spiral shell, but without the tiger stripes.

14 Paint in the coral using the chisel edge of a no. 6 flat brush loaded with Burnt Carmine and Wicker White.

15 To add shadows next to the shells, load a no. 12 flat with Floating Medium, then side load into Burnt Umber. Hold the Burnt Umber against the shell design and float a soft-edged shadow to give depth and dimension. Do the same on the other side of the shells. Then repeat this entire design on the opposite side of the lid.

Corals and Shells on Front

16 After tracing the pattern onto the front of the trunk, use a dampened household sponge stroked into Butter Pecan on one edge to shade in the sand line.

17 With inky Gray Plum on a no. 2 script liner, paint all the veins into the fan coral. Start from the base and pull to the outer edge.

18 Double load Gray Plum and Gold Reflecting Medium (or Inca Gold Metallic) on a ¾-inch (19mm) flat. Paint the outer edge of the fan coral all the way around (keeping the Gray Plum to the outside), then fill in the middle.

19 Double load a no. 12 flat with Burnt Carmine and Gray Plum, dip into a little Floating Medium, and paint branching coral outward from behind the shell design.

20 With a ¾-inch (19mm) flat loaded with Wicker White and a little Berry Wine, hold the white to the outer rippled edge of the conch shell opening. Stroke the Berry Wine along the bottom edge of the opening for depth. Stroke back and forth in the middle to fill in, working to shade the area from dark to light. Add two clam shells the same way you did on the top of the lid.

21 Following your pattern, start at the tip of the cone area of the shell and outline your layers with Mushroom and Wicker White and a touch of Burnt Umber. Make the points along the edge of the shell with the flat of the brush.

22 Continue painting the bottom of the conch shell with Mushroom, Wicker White and a touch of Burnt Umber.

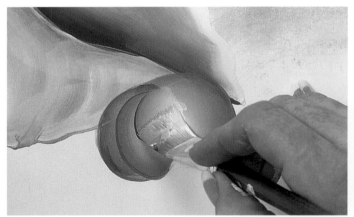

23 Using a no. 12 flat loaded with Gray Plum and Wicker White, pick up a touch of Dark Plum and paint C-strokes to form outer edges. Fill in with more segments.

24 With a no. 2 script liner, dot in details with Dark Plum and the circle at the top with Burnt Carmine.

25 For the pointed-end shell, double load Terra Cotta and Wicker White on a ¾-inch (19mm) flat. Paint C-strokes, starting small and getting bigger as you near the top of the shell.

26 For the large spiral shell, use the same brush and load Mushroom and Wicker White, plus Floating Medium. Paint the back of the shell first, then the front edge.

27 Double load a no. 12 flat with Burnt Umber and Floating Medium and shade the inside of the shell opening, holding Burnt Umber to the outer edge.

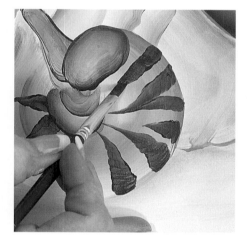

28 With a no. 6 flat and Burnt Sienna, paint the stripes from the outer edge toward the center.

29 Load a ¾-inch (19mm) flat with Floating Medium, side load into Burnt Umber, and add shading around the design. Hold the Burnt Umber against the shell edges.

30 Complete the design by shading around the rest of the shells using the same brush.

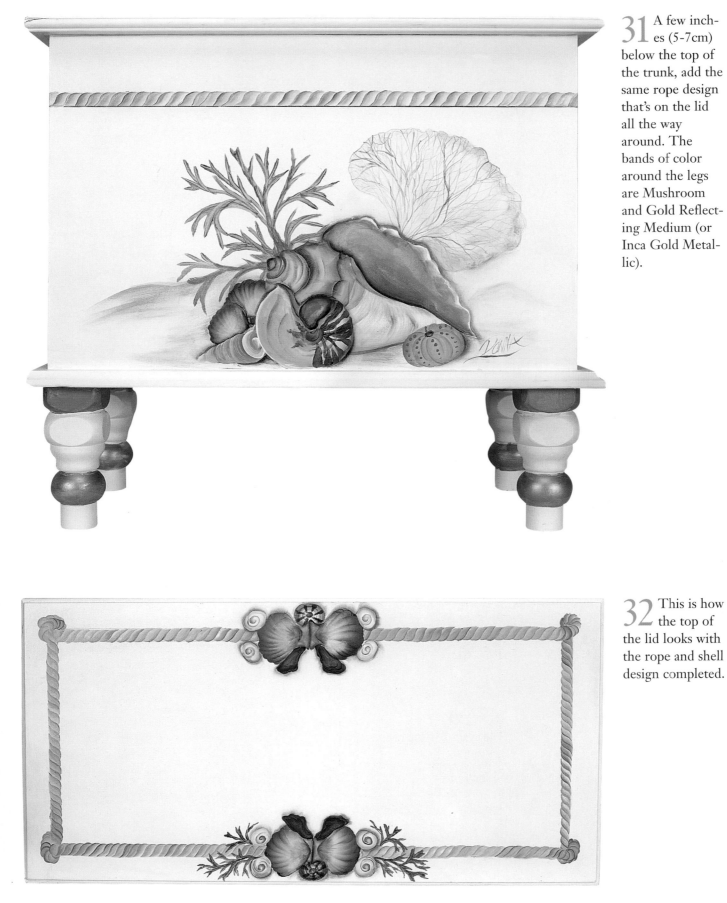

31 A few inches (5-7cm) below the top of the trunk, add the same rope design that's on the lid all the way around. The bands of color around the legs are Mushroom and Gold Reflecting Medium (or Inca Gold Metallic).

32 This is how the top of the lid looks with the rope and shell design completed.

Patterns for Sea Shell Trunk

These patterns may be hand-traced or photocopied for personal use only. Enlarge the top one (for the front of the trunk) at 286% and the bottom one (for the lid) at 152% to bring them up to full size.

Floral Jewelry Armoire

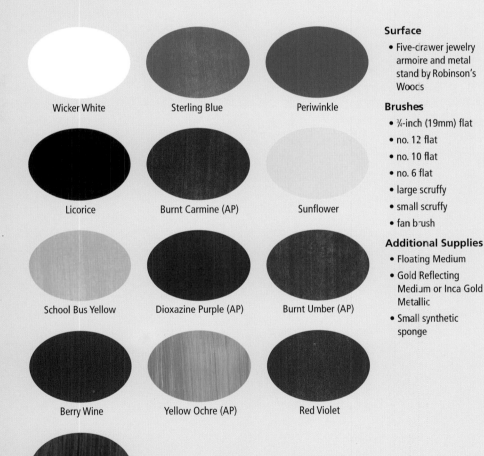

MATERIALS

PAINT: FolkArt by Plaid   **(AP) = FolkArt Artists' Pigment**

Wicker White	Sterling Blue	Periwinkle
Licorice	Burnt Carmine (AP)	Sunflower
School Bus Yellow	Dioxazine Purple (AP)	Burnt Umber (AP)
Berry Wine	Yellow Ochre (AP)	Red Violet
Green Forest		

Surface
- Five-drawer jewelry armoire and metal stand by Robinson's Woods

Brushes
- ¾-inch (19mm) flat
- no. 12 flat
- no. 10 flat
- no. 6 flat
- large scruffy
- small scruffy
- fan brush

Additional Supplies
- Floating Medium
- Gold Reflecting Medium or Inca Gold Metallic
- Small synthetic sponge

I love having lots of little drawers to fill with all my favorite jewelry. I painted this little dresser top armoire with everything I enjoy in nature — wildflowers, grasses, and cute little garden insects. Shiny brass pulls on the drawer fronts give a nice finishing touch.

Background and Foliage

1 Double load a small round dampened sponge with Sterling Blue and Wicker White. I like a synthetic sponge better than a sea sponge, the smaller holes give a better effect. Don't ever put one color on first, then sponge on the second — always double load your sponge.

2 Make circular motions with the sponge to quickly fill in the background.

3 Pounce with the sponge (double loaded with more Sterling Blue and Wicker White) randomly over the still-wet paint. Let the background dry before going on.

4 Following the pattern, use a ¾-inch (19mm) flat multiloaded with Green Forest, White Wicker, a touch of Sunflower plus Floating Medium. You want this to be light and transparent looking. Paint all the grass stems and large shadow leaves.

5 Double load a no. 6 flat with Dioxazine Purple and Wicker White. Starting at the top of each stem, paint short strokes (staying up on the chisel edge of the brush) to form lavender blossoms. On this flower, I led with the purple edge of my brush.

Pink Blossoms

6 With a ¾-inch (19mm) flat multi-loaded with Green Forest, Wicker White and Sunflower, paint in larger leaves. Use a no. 10 flat double loaded with Berry Wine and Wicker White to paint the pink blossoms, keeping the white toward the rippled outside edge of the petals.

7 Add centers to the pink blossoms with Burnt Carmine and Yellow Ochre double loaded on a small scruffy brush. Pounce in the centers, holding the Burnt Carmine side of the brush upward.

8 Using a no. 2 script liner with inky Green Forest, connect each blossom to the stem. On the same brush, pick up Green Forest and Sunflower and pull little stamens into the centers.

Black-Eyed Susans

9 Paint more green stems in with a no. 12 flat double loaded with Sunflower and Green Forest, pulling downward from top to bottom. Paint the black-eyed Susan petals with School Bus Yellow, Yellow Ochre and Wicker White on a no. 12 flat. Stay up on the chisel edge and pull each stroke from the outside toward the center.

10 Pounce on the centers with Burnt Carmine and Yellow Ochre double loaded on a small scruffy brush.

11 Add small leaves here and there among the blossoms with Green Forest and Sunflower on a no. 12 flat.

Wildflowers and Grasses

12 For the wild violets mixed in among the pink blossoms, use Periwinkle and Wicker White with Floating Medium to make little C-stroke petals, holding the white to the outer edge. Dot with School Bus Yellow for the centers.

13 Double load a no. 12 flat with Green Forest and Wicker White, then pick up a little Sunflower and Floating Medium. Paint the filler leaves in the center, then pull stems into these leaves. With a large scruffy brush multi-loaded with Green Forest, Wicker White and Sunflower, pounce on mounds of moss at the base. Let the moss dry before going on.

14 Load a no. 2 script liner with inky Green Forest and paint in some wild grasses, pulling upward from the moss. To paint the Queen Anne's lace, load both sides of a fan brush into Wicker White, then stroke the brush gently across a puddle of Berry Wine. Lightly tap the bristles in a fan shape to form light, airy-looking blossoms.

15 Fill the flowers with all kinds of little insects normally found in a field of wildflowers.

16 For the pink sedum, double load a no. 10 flat with Wicker White and Berry Wine. Tap the chisel edge in a fan shape, making several layers. Using a no. 2 script liner and inky Green Forest, paint little connecting stemlets under each blossom.

Thistles on Side Panels

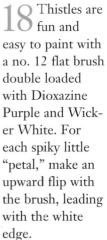

18 Thistles are fun and easy to paint with a no. 12 flat brush double loaded with Dioxazine Purple and Wicker White. For each spiky little "petal," make an upward flip with the brush, leading with the white edge.

17 If you wish, continue the wildflower theme onto the side panels of the jewelry armoire. Paint in some grasses and leaves and pounce moss just as you did on the front. Here I used more Floating Medium on my brush to make the stems look more subtle and like they're in the background. I then added a few different types of flowers such as daisies, ragweed and veronica before I began painting the thistles.

19 Using a no. 6 flat double loaded with Sunflower and Green Forest, paint the base of the thistles with a curvy U-stroke, keeping the green edge at the bottom. Then make three little leaves hanging down from that base.

20 With the same flat brush, make tiny downward strokes in layers all the way to the stem, leading with the Green Forest edge of the brush.

Add Little Garden Insects

21 Finish off the side panels with any other wildflowers you like and maybe even a bumblebee or other garden critters.

22 On the top of the armoire, paint little butterflies, dragonflies and bumblebees so they look like they're hovering over the garden on the front of the armoire. Refer to pages 43-45 for instructions on painting insects and suggested colors.

Pattern for Front of Armoire

This pattern may be hand-traced or photocopied for personal use only. Enlarge at 238% to bring it up to full size.

Finished Jewelry Armoire

23 Add some small, bright brass drawer pulls to give your jewelry armoire an elegant finished look.

Lavender & Hydrangeas on Stackable Drawers

MATERIALS

PAINT: FolkArt by Plaid　　**(AP) = FolkArt Artists' Pigment**

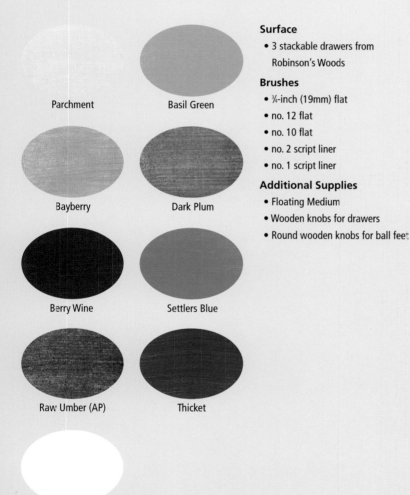

Parchment

Basil Green

Bayberry

Dark Plum

Berry Wine

Settlers Blue

Raw Umber (AP)

Thicket

Wicker White

Surface
- 3 stackable drawers from Robinson's Woods

Brushes
- ¾-inch (19mm) flat
- no. 12 flat
- no. 10 flat
- no. 2 script liner
- no. 1 script liner

Additional Supplies
- Floating Medium
- Wooden knobs for drawers
- Round wooden knobs for ball feet

I bought these stackable wooden drawer units in three different sizes for a lighter, more contemporary look. To separate the pieces, I added ball feet in progressively larger sizes to the bottom of each unit. All sides of the drawer units were basecoated first with two coats of Parchment, sanding between each coat. Then I transferred the patterns for the hydrangeas to the drawer fronts and for the lavender to the top unit. These stackable drawers would be a handy place to keep your scrapbooking collections, old photos, and supplies.

Hydrangeas

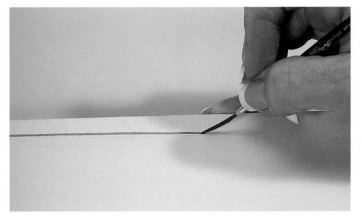

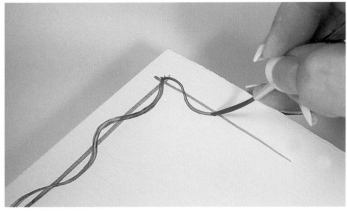

1 Pin-stripe the top of each drawer cabinet using a no. 2 script liner with inky Thicket. Drag the liner behind your hand, bracing your little finger along the edge to help you gauge the placement of the pinstripe.

2 Then freehand a wavy line over the pinstripe. This acts as a kind of frame for the lavender you'll be painting on the top of the highest set of drawers.

3 Paint a hydrangea leaf with Basil and Bayberry on one corner of a ¾-inch (19mm) flat and Dark Plum on the other corner. Keep the Dark Plum to the inside of the leaf. Watch the outer edge of the leaf: slide the brush in and out to give a ripply edge. Then pull a stem into the leaf.

4 With a no. 10 flat loaded with Settlers Blue and Floating Medium, make individual hydrangea petals, layering the florets over each other.

5 With the same brush, dip one corner into Dark Plum and paint a few petals, then dip into Berry Wine and paint a few more. A variety of colors looks more natural.

6 Dot in centers on some of the florets with a no. 1 script liner dipped into Bayberry, then stroked across Thicket. Add curlicues with inky Bayberry to finish.

Lavender

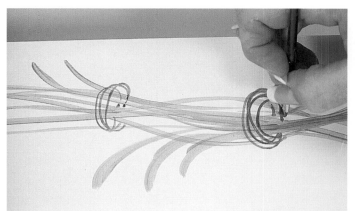

7 To paint the lavender on the top of the highest drawer, double load a ¾-inch (19mm) flat with Basil Green and Thicket, then pick up Floating Medium. Pull some softly curved stems upward, then add long comma strokes to form foliage.

8 With a no. 2 script liner and inky Raw Umber, paint some loops to tie the stems together at the bottom and then again partway up.

9 To form the lavender blossoms, multi-load a no. 12 flat with Dark Plum, Wicker White and Floating Medium. Use the chisel edge of the brush to paint short strokes downward toward the stems.

10 With the same brush, pick up Berry Wine on the Dark Plum corner and add more strokes for color variation in the blossoms.

11 Finally, pick up Dark Plum on the Berry Wine corner of the same brush and add even darker petals.

Patterns for Hydrangeas and Lavender

These patterns may be hand-traced or photocopied for personal use only. Enlarge the top one at 119% and the bottom two at 244% to bring them up to full size.

Finish

12 Repeat the lavender design on the opposite side, varying the shape of the lavender and the colors. It's the little variations like these that give your furniture pieces that hand-painted look.

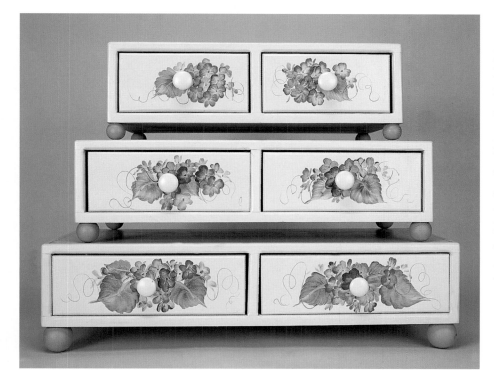

13 This is how the drawer fronts look with all of the completed hydrangeas. Notice how the clusters of hydrangeas and leaves get larger and more numerous the larger the drawer gets.

The drawer pulls and ball feet are just plain wooden knobs that can be bought at a home improvement center. The ball feet come in small, medium and large sizes. Basecoat the ball feet with Basil Green and let dry completely before attaching. The drawer pulls are just basecoated with Parchment. Add tiny flowers to the knobs if you wish.

Tropical Birdhouse Cabinet

MATERIALS

PAINT: FolkArt by Plaid **(AP) = FolkArt Artists' Pigment**

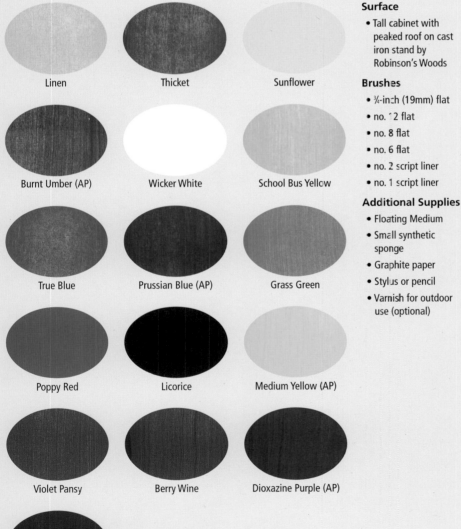

Linen

Thicket

Sunflower

Burnt Umber (AP)

Wicker White

School Bus Yellow

True Blue

Prussian Blue (AP)

Grass Green

Poppy Red

Licorice

Medium Yellow (AP)

Violet Pansy

Berry Wine

Dioxazine Purple (AP)

Burnt Carmine (AP)

Surface
• Tall cabinet with peaked roof on cast iron stand by Robinson's Woods

Brushes
• ¾-inch (19mm) flat
• no. 12 flat
• no. 8 flat
• no. 6 flat
• no. 2 script liner
• no. 1 script liner

Additional Supplies
• Floating Medium
• Small synthetic sponge
• Graphite paper
• Stylus or pencil
• Varnish for outdoor use (optional)

his tall wooden cabinet with its peaked roof and tropical look is perfect for outdoor use, such as in a sunroom or a screened-in porch, on the patio, or next to the pool. If you plan to keep this cabinet outdoors, protect the painting with a varnish specially formulated for exterior use.

Branches and Green Parrot

1 Load a ¾-inch (19mm) flat with Floating Medium, then work a little Thicket and Linen well into the brush. Paint the fern stems for positioning, pulling each frond from the stem outward. Load a no. 8 flat with Thicket and Floating Medium and paint little clusters of one-stroke shadow leaves. Repeat around the cabinet where desired and on the bottom shelf.

2 Double load a ¾-inch (19mm) flat with Wicker White and Burnt Umber to paint the branches. The movement is the same as painting vines, but putting more pressure on the chisel edge of the brush makes the branches thicker than vines. Pay attention to the way the smaller branches come off of a larger branch — never at a 90-degree angle.

3 Begin the green parrot by tracing on the pattern. Paint the head with a no. 12 flat loaded with School Bus Yellow and side loaded into Poppy Red. Stroke the outer edge of the head first, then fill in. Load a no. 8 flat with Wicker White and Medium Yellow and paint the eye area with two wavy circles for the wrinkles.

4 With a ¾-inch (19mm) flat, pick up Grass Green and Medium Yellow. Start down at the end of the longest tail feather and paint long, chisel-edge strokes up toward the body to represent tail feathers.

5 To paint the left wing, add Thicket to the same brush and stroke the wing feathers over the tail feathers, starting from the outer tip of the wing and working upward toward the shoulder. The green will get progressively darker as you pick up more Thicket on your brush.

6 Wipe excess paint out of your brush onto a paper towel. Pick up a little Wicker White and add a row of white feathers, again stroking from the wing tip toward the body. With the same brush, pick up Grass Green and Medium Yellow and finish the rest of the feathers up to the shoulder.

7 To paint the right wing, start at the outer tip again and overlay strokes right on top of the wing you already painted, using a ¾-inch (19mm) flat with Grass Green and Medium Yellow.

8 Alternate feather colors all the way up to the shoulder, adding Wicker White, then Thicket and Medium Yellow feathers. With a no. 6 flat double loaded with Thicket and Grass Green, paint the bottom part of the beak, holding Thicket toward the edge of the beak.

9 For the top of the beak, pick up Medium Yellow and Thicket on the same brush. Stroke the yellow edge first, then paint the top edge of the top beak, holding Thicket to the outer edge.

10 Load a no. 1 script liner with Licorice and paint the circle for the eye, the line that separates the beak from the head, and the nostril. Dip the tip of the same brush into Wicker White and add highlights to all those areas. Load a no. 2 script liner with inky Licorice and detail some wavy lines around the eyes.

Parrots and White Orchid

11 Load a ¾-inch (19mm) flat with Floating Medium and side load into Burnt Umber. Float some shading around the green parrot.

12 To paint the bright blue parrot, load a ¾-inch (19mm) flat with True Blue and Prussian Blue and a little Wicker White. Paint the head, body and tail feathers first. Next paint the back wing, then the front wing, with Grass Green, School Bus Yellow and Wicker White. The wing feathers are painted the same way as for the green parrot, starting at the tip and stroking toward the shoulder. The beak colors are Prussian Blue and True Blue.

13 Begin the white orchid by loading a ¾-inch (19mm) flat with Wicker White and a touch of Medium Yellow; side load the white corner into a little Berry Wine. Paint the back upper petal — sliding up to a point, changing direction of bristles and sliding back down, keeping pink to the outer edge. Paint the two side petals by putting pressure on the bristles and making loopy, wiggling strokes to make the pink edges look ruffly.

14 Load Wicker White and a little Medium Yellow on a no. 12 flat and paint the bottom two petals, sliding down to a point and back up in one stroke.

15 Add Grass Green to the same brush and paint some green veins from the center outward, using the chisel edge of your brush. Let all the petals dry.

16 Load a no. 12 flat with Floating Medium, then side load into Grass Green. Float some shading around the edges of the large side petals.

17 For the trumpet part of the orchid, load School Bus Yellow and Berry Wine on a no. 12 flat to paint the base of the trumpet. Pick up Wicker White on the School Bus Yellow corner of the brush and start painting ruffles around the opening of the trumpet.

18 Before completing the circle of ruffles, paint a Berry Wine scoop underneath, then finish the ruffly petals.

19 With the same brush, make little strokes from inside the trumpet's throat downward toward the ruffly edge, leading with the yellow corner of the brush. Let dry.

20 Load a no. 6 flat with Floating Medium, side load into Berry Wine, and add a little shading accent at the throat for depth.

21 Add a little touch of white to the throat after finishing the dark shading accent.

22 With Thicket and a bit of Sunflower on a ¾-inch (19mm) flat, pull a stem from the back of the orchid to the branch, then paint some large smooth leaves, keeping Thicket to the outside edges.

Purple, Pink and Yellow Orchids

23 The purple orchids are painted in much the same way as the white orchid, but the colors are Violet Pansy and Dioxazine Purple, plus Berry Wine. The centers and leaves are Thicket and School Bus Yellow.

24 The colors for the pink orchids are Burnt Carmine, Wicker White and School Bus Yellow for the outer petals, and School Bus Yellow, Thicket and Wicker White for the centers.

25 The yellow flowers are School Bus Yellow and Wicker White for the petals; Burnt Carmine for the centers; and Grass Green and Yellow for the stems.

26 Dampen a small synthetic sponge and multi-load it with Wicker White, Sunflower, Thicket, and Burnt Umber. Sponge some moss on the roof and under the eaves. Finish with some small leaves painted with Thicket and Floating Medium.

Pattern For Tropical Birds and Orchids

This pattern may be hand-traced or photocopied for personal use only. Enlarge at 303% to bring it up to full size.

Finished Cabinet

Completed Cabinet
Front

Left Side Panel

Right Side Panel

Wildflowers and Ferns on Tray Table

MATERIALS

PAINT: FolkArt by Plaid   **(AP) = FolkArt Artists' Pigment**

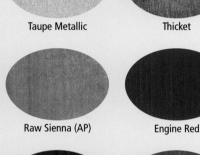

Wicker White   Taupe Metallic   Thicket

Raw Umber (AP)   Raw Sienna (AP)   Engine Red

Yellow Ochre (AP) Burnt Carmine (AP)   Burnt Sienna (AP)

Berry Wine   Dark Plum

Surface
- Folding tray table by Country Pleasures

Brushes
- ¾-inch (19mm) flat
- no. 12 flat
- no. 2 script liner
- no. 1 script liner

Additional Supplies
- Floating Medium
- Plastic wrap
- Butter Pecan (optional)
- Inca Gold Metallic (optional)
- Waterbased satin varnish

Tray tables usually look kind of plain and functional, but here's one that is elegant and substantial enough to use as a coffee table. I began by basecoating the table and the folding legs white. Then I added a "faux finish" using plastic wrap and Taupe Metallic for a richer look. If you can't find this color, use a mix of Butter Pecan and Inca Gold Metallic for a similar effect. Paint the bottom of each folding table leg with a metallic color. Finish off the table top with little bright brass knobs on each side to dress it up.

Pattern for Wildflowers and Ferns

This pattern may be hand-traced or photocopied for personal use only. Enlarge at 263% to bring it up to full size.

Grapevines and Ferns

1 Double load a ¾-inch (19mm) flat brush with Raw Umber and Wicker White, then dip it into Floating Medium. Paint the grapevine around the perimeter of the table top, staying up on the chisel edge of the brush and leading with the white corner. Keep a loose, open design.

To add some fern fronds on each side of the table top, use the same brush and dip it in Thicket. Paint fern stems first for placement. Then with the same colors loaded onto a no. 12 flat, pull in the fern leaves toward the stem, lifting up to the chisel edge as you near the stem.

2 Paint shadow leaves here and there with the same brush. Pull stems into each leaf from the grapevine.

3 Using a ¾-inch (19mm) flat double loaded with Raw Sienna and Thicket, pick up a little Raw Umber and Floating Medium on the brush. Paint the large leaves in each of the corners, keeping the Thicket to the outer edge.

Maple Leaf

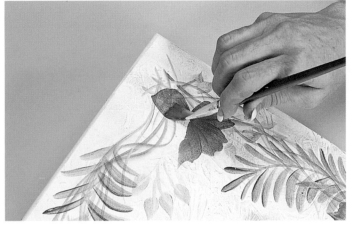

4 Add Burnt Sienna and Thicket to the same ¾-inch (19mm) flat you just used for the large leaves. Paint a large maple leaf in one corner by wiggling your brush out to the point of the leaf, then sliding back to center. Keep Thicket to the outside edge.

5 Continue to wiggle the brush back out to the next point and slide back to center, making sure you're watching the green edge of the leaf at all times to keep the shape right.

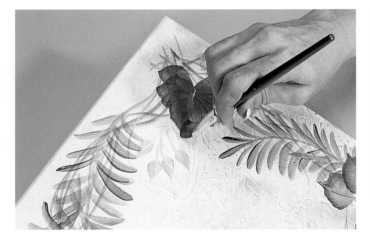

6 Push down hard on the bristles, wiggle and turn the green side of the brush to the tip of the leaf.

7 Pull a stem into the center of the leaf with the same brush, staying up on the chisel edge and painting wet-into-wet.

8 Again, using the same brush, add some veins in the maple leaf by pulling from the outside edge of the leaf into the center. Stay up on the chisel edge of the brush to get these fine lines.

Flowers

9 These trumpet flowers are easy to paint. Double load your no. 12 flat with Raw Sienna and Wicker White and stroke in the back portion of each blossom.

10 Double load the same brush with Burnt Sienna and a little Berry Wine and stroke in the front portion.

11 Add in some purple, pink, yellow and white blossoms wherever you like. These are the same easy-to-paint, five-petal flowers shown in Project 3. For the purple flowers, double load your no. 12 flat with Dark Plum and Wicker White. For the pink flowers, double load with Engine Red and Wicker White. The yellow flowers are Yellow Ochre and Wicker White. And the white flowers start out with Wicker White and a touch of Raw Umber. The flowers below the maple leaf are white flowers with Burnt Sienna and a touch of Berry Wine for shading.

Detail the Flowers

12 On the white flowers, load your brush with Floating Medium and Raw Umber and shade the petals so the white edges look like they curl up and over.

13 Use inky Wicker White on a no. 2 script liner to pull short stamens in each white flower's center all the way around.

14 Dot Burnt Carmine in the center. Use a no. 2 script liner loaded with Wicker White and dipped into Yellow Ochre to dot the ends of the little stamens.

15 The centers of the yellow blossoms begin with five little strokes inward, using a no. 1 script liner loaded with Yellow Ochre.

16 Using the same brush, pull shorter strokes of Burnt Sienna toward the center on each yellow blossom.

17 Finally, dot the center with Thicket on the end of your brush handle.

18 Detail the centers of all the flowers using the same general method and whatever colors look good to you. Remember, these are just for fun — there's no need to be botanically accurate. To finish off the table top, I added my signature, then sealed it with a waterbased satin varnish.

Trompe L'oeil Folding Screen

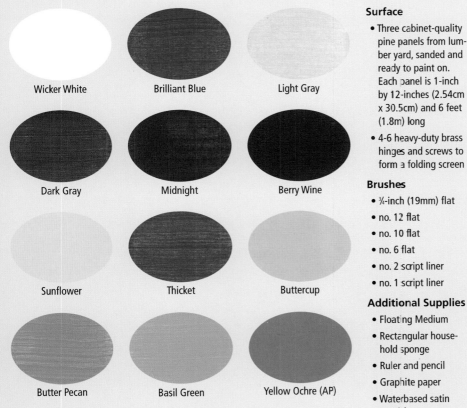

MATERIALS

PAINT: FolkArt by Plaid   **(AP) = FolkArt Artists' Pigment**

Wicker White

Brilliant Blue

Light Gray

Dark Gray

Midnight

Berry Wine

Sunflower

Thicket

Buttercup

Butter Pecan

Basil Green

Yellow Ochre (AP)

Surface

- Three cabinet-quality pine panels from lumber yard, sanded and ready to paint on. Each panel is 1-inch by 12-inches (2.54cm x 30.5cm) and 6 feet (1.8m) long
- 4-6 heavy-duty brass hinges and screws to form a folding screen

Brushes

- ¾-inch (19mm) flat
- no. 12 flat
- no. 10 flat
- no. 6 flat
- no. 2 script liner
- no. 1 script liner

Additional Supplies

- Floating Medium
- Rectangular household sponge
- Ruler and pencil
- Graphite paper
- Waterbased satin varnish

A folding screen can help divide space in a room, dress up a plain corner, or hide an unsightly area. I painted this folding screen in a trompe l'oeil fashion to make it look like a large wall cabinet. The blue-and-white china and the books remind me of my family's collectibles and journals. This screen started out as three pine panels that I sanded and basecoated with Wicker White. When the basecoat was dry, I transferred each pattern to its proper place, then began painting the trompe l'oeil cabinet.

Patterns for Yellow Flowers, Lace Doily, and Blue & White China

This pattern may be hand-traced or photocopied for personal use only. Enlarge at 263% to bring it up to full size.

Trompe L'oeil Shelves & Lace Doily

1 Starting with the upper left portion of the lefthand panel, use a ruler and pencil to lightly sketch in the sides and the shelves in a configuration you like. Make sure all the components (doors, curves, etc.) match in width.

Stroke one edge of a dampened household sponge into Butter Pecan. Draw the lines of the trompe l'oeil cabinet and shelves and shade them at the same time with the sponge. Note how there's more shading under the shelves and in the corners.

2 To paint the lace doily, thinly basecoat the doily area with Wicker White. (If it's too opaque the shelf won't show through the "fabric.") Load a no. 10 flat with Wicker White and Light Gray and paint scallops around the pointed edge of the doily.

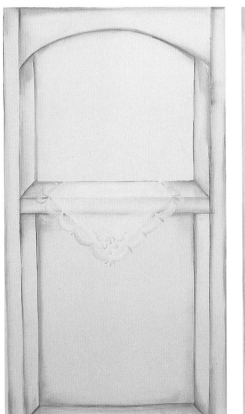

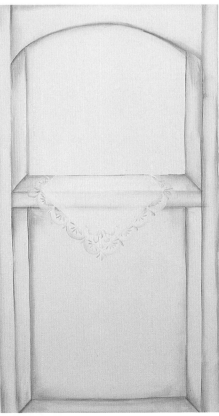

3 With the same brush, paint little details in the corner lace. Add little embroidered accents around the outer edge.

4 In each scallop, paint a sunburst detail.

Lace Doily and China Vase

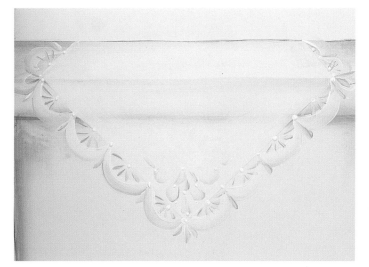

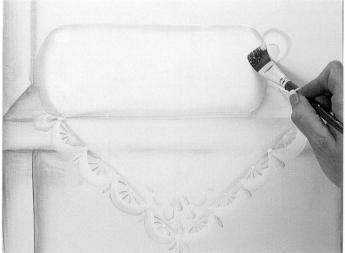

5 Dot in Wicker White with the end of your brush handle to represent knots.

6 Basecoat the bowl shape of the vase with Wicker White. Load a ¾-inch (19mm) flat with Floating Medium and side load into Light Gray. Shade around all edges, keeping the gray to the outside.

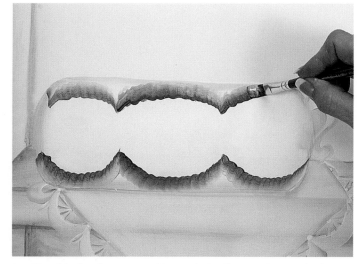

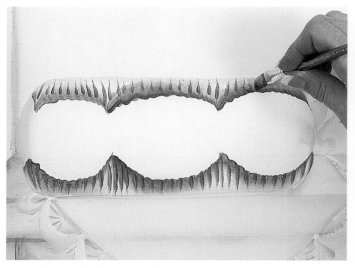

7 Double load a no. 12 flat with Brilliant Blue and Floating Medium. Wiggle on scallops along the top and bottom edges, keeping the blue side of the brush toward the middle of the bowl.

8 Pick up a little Midnight on the same brush and stroke little lines up from the bottom scallops and down from the top scallops. Stay up on the chisel edge of your brush for these lines.

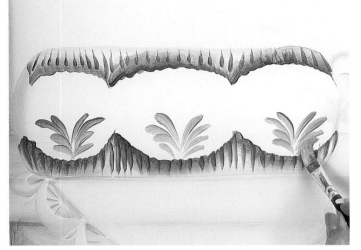

9 Add a little Wicker White and more Floating Medium to the same brush and make light blue comma strokes in the bottom scallops.

10 With a no. 2 script liner loaded with inky Brilliant Blue and Midnight, add crosshatching to the bottom scallops and wiggly lines under the top scallops.

11 Add rosebuds and one-stroke leaves with Midnight and Floating Medium loaded on a no. 6 flat brush. Detail the handle with linework and outline the top and bottom edges of the vase with a script liner.

12 Double load a ¾-inch (19mm) flat with Thicket and Sunflower. Paint the large leaves for the bouquet and pull stems upward into them. Paint a few extra stems laying on the "shelf."

Yellow Flowers and Scrollwork

14 Double load a no. 6 flat with Light Gray and Dark Gray and pick up some Floating Medium. Add "wrought iron" scrollwork accents on both sides of the curved area.

13 Add yellow five-petal flowers with Buttercup and Wicker White double loaded on a no. 12 flat. Paint some of the blossoms with white outer edges and some with yellow outer edges for variety. Add shading lines with inky Yellow Ochre. Dot in centers with Yellow Ochre and Thicket.

15 This is how the top left part of the panel looks so far.

Blue & White China Platter

16 Now let's move down to the middle shelf of the lefthand panel, where I've painted a trompe l'oeil china platter.

Begin by basecoating the oval area with Wicker White on a ¾-inch (19mm) flat. Side load the same brush into Light Gray and shade the center of the platter. Paint the rim with Brilliant Blue and Wicker White plus Floating Medium on a no. 10 flat. Use inky Midnight on a script liner to paint freehand Xs and to outline the blue rim.

17 Load a no. 12 flat with Brilliant Blue and Floating Medium and paint a vine around the edge of the plate.

18 Paint a large cabbage rose in the center with Brilliant Blue and Midnight on a ¾-inch (19mm) flat. Load a no. 12 flat with the same colors for the smaller roses at each side and the buds in the center.

19 Add the large leaves with Brilliant Blue and Floating Medium on a ¾-inch (19mm) flat. The medium leaves are painted with Midnight and Floating Medium on a no. 12 flat, and the smallest leaves are painted with a no. 6 flat.

20 Add little one-stroke leaves all around the rim of the platter. To add depth and realism, shade underneath the platter and under the lace edge of the doily with Butter Pecan and Floating Medium.

Trompe L'oeil Door and Birdcage

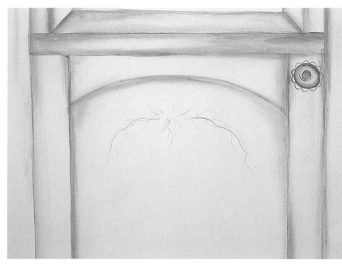

21 Paint a subtle garland design on the cabinet "door" using a script liner and inky Butter Pecan to place the vines. The doorknob is detailed with inky Dark Gray.

22 Load a no. 10 flat with Butter Pecan and Floating Medium and paint little one-stroke leaves, connecting them to the vines. With the same brush, pick up more Floating Medium and stroke on subtle shadow leaves in the background.

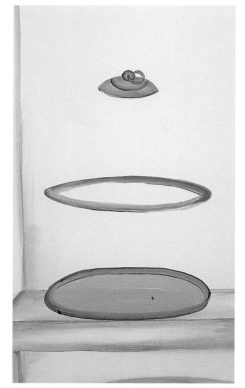

23 Begin the birdcage by basecoating the bottom circle and top circle with Light Gray. Add Dark Gray to the same brush and paint the rim on the bottom and center circles. Detail the top with a no. 1 script liner.

24 Load a no. 2 script liner with inky Dark Gray and freehand the wires from top to bottom. Make sure some touch the back edge of the bottom circle and some touch the front. This gives a rounded look to the birdcage.

25 Add some vines with Thicket and Sunflower on a ¾-inch (19mm) flat. Don't worry if your birdcage wires are not perfect — you can always wind your vines to cover any spot you don't like.

26 Add leaves in a variety of sizes draped over and around the birdcage. Double load Thicket and Sunflower on a ¾-inch (19mm) flat for the largest, ripply-edged leaves. Fill in with smooth-edged, one-stroke leaves using a no. 12 flat, then use a no. 2 script liner with inky Thicket for new growth tendrils.

27 To finish off the lefthand panel of the screen, detail the cabinet "door" with more shading to give a raised panel effect. Let the leaves from the shelf above hang gracefully over the door, and make the doorknob as fancy or as simple as you wish.

Pattern for Pink Tulips in Blue & White Planter

This pattern may be hand-traced or photocopied for personal use only. Enlarge at
263% to bring it up to full size.

Pink Tulips

28 Double load a ¾-inch (19mm) flat with Berry Wine and Wicker White; dip the Wicker White corner into Sunflower. Wiggle the brush upward and stop at the point of the petal. Don't lift your brush up off the surface yet.

29 Now lean the brush down, reverse direction and wiggle down to finish the petal. Both steps 28 and 29 are done in one stroke. Be sure you've kept the Berry Wine toward the center.

30 To layer petals, wiggle up to the tip and slide down, leading with the Berry Wine edge of the brush.

31 Wiggle the brush up on the opposite side and slide it down again on the chisel edge.

32 Wiggle up and back down one more time for the center petal. Add a hanging petal by wiggling down to the point and sliding back up to the base of the tulip.

33 With a ¾-inch (19mm) flat loaded with Thicket and Sunflower, paint the top of the stem and the base of the tulip. Then pull the stem down into the flower pot.

34 For the leaves, make sure your brush has plenty of paint (Thicket and Sunflower) and Floating Medium (almost dripping). Start the leaf from the bottom, stroke upward on the chisel edge, then press down on the bristles as you're moving upward to form the wider part of the leaf. Lift back up to chisel edge, then press down on the bristles to the other side to form another wide area, then lift again to the chisel edge to form the point of the leaf.

35 To make a folded leaf, start up on the chisel edge of your brush, press the bristles down to one side to widen the leaf, raise up to the chisel edge and flip the brush over to form the fold.

36 For a more realistic look, make some of the tulips buds, some open and some past their prime. Add moss to the planter, then pull stems down into the moss.

Books and Lower Door

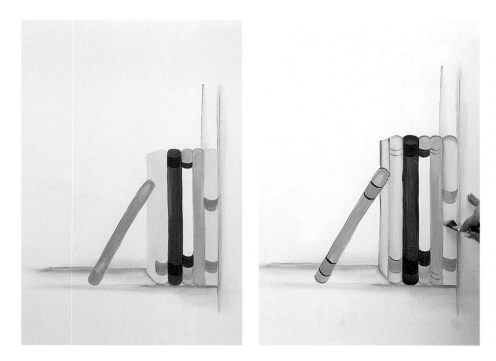

37 What's a trompe l'oeil cabinet without a few books stacked up here and there? Take a look at your own bookshelves to see how the perspective works. Then basecoat on some different colors to make each book distinctive. Here I used Sunflower, Berry Wine mixed with Wicker White, Brilliant Blue, Butter Pecan and Basil Green.

38 To give dimension to the bindings, load a ¼-inch (19mm) flat with Floating Medium and a darker shade of each book's basecoat color. Float shading around each book, keeping the color to the outside edge. Use a script liner to add detail on the spines.

39 Use a script liner to freehand in any book titles that you like, or that are meaningful. Float Butter Pecan under and along the back edges of the books to separate them from the shelves.

40 The "door" underneath the books on this part of the screen is painted the same way as the other door. Refer to pages 114-115 for instructions. Don't forget to place the knob on the opposite side this time.

Pattern for Books

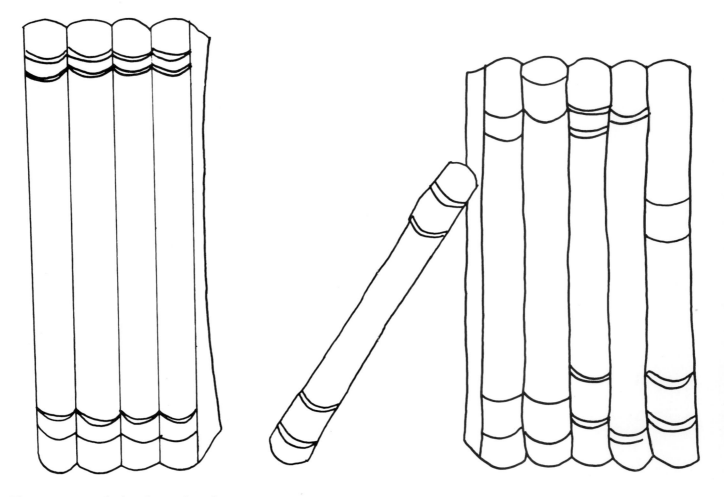

This pattern may be hand-traced or photo-copied for personal use only. Enlarge at 222% to bring it up to full size.

Tea Cups and Plate

41 On the shelf above the books is another set of blue-and-white china with yellow flowers. These tea cups and plate are painted with the same colors as for the vase and oval platter shown on pages 110-111 and 113. The lace-edged doily is only slightly different from the one shown earlier. To give form and dimension to the tea cups, shade inside the rim with Dark Gray and Floating Medium. Shade under the plate too, and add yellow blossoms to one tea cup.

Pattern for Blue & White China Tea Pot

This pattern may be hand-traced or photo-copied for personal use only. Enlarge at 127% to bring it up to full size.

Blue & White China Tea Pot

42 The topmost shelf of the righthand panel holds a china tea pot sitting on another lacy doily with some yellow blossoms. Although the patterns are a little different, these elements are painted the same way and with the same colors as shown on pages 110-111. Don't forget to shade inside the spout opening and under the tea pot with Dark Gray and Floating Medium.

Pattern for Plate Hangers

This pattern may be hand-traced or photocopied for personal use only. Enlarge at 217% to bring it up to full size.

Plate Hangers

43 Here's another set of china plates displayed on wire "plate hangers." The easiest way to paint these is, before the plates are based in, paint in all the wire plate hangers except the pieces that hold the plate rims. Then paint both plates completely, then finish the hangers over the plate rims. The wire hangers are painted with Dark Gray and Floating Medium on a ¾-inch (19mm) flat brush. The plates are painted with the same colors used for the vase and oval platter shown on pages 110-111 and 113. If you have a collection of blue-and-white china at home, try copying some of the patterns for this screen (but practice first on a piece of scrap board).

Finished Trompe L'oeil Screen

Once all the panels are completely painted, give them a protective coat of waterbased satin varnish. If you want to paint something different on the backs of the panels to give you a reversible screen, wait until all painting is finished before you varnish. Then attach the panels with good, strong brass hinges, using two or three per panel. Be sure each panel is in the right position before you hinge them together.

Resources

Plaid Enterprises
3225 Westech Drive
Norcross, GA 30092
Phone (678) 291-8100
FAX (678) 291-8156
www.plaidonline.com

Cabin Crafters
1225 W. First St.
Nevada, IA 50201
Phone (800) 669-3920
FAX (515) 382-3106
www.cabincrafters.com

Robinson's Woods
1057 Trumbull Ave.
Unit N
Girard, OH 44420
Phone (800) 445-7028

Country Pleasures
10003 CR 6310
West Plains, MO 65775
Phone (417) 256-5828

Dry Grass Collection
by Jeff McWilliams
5965 Peachtree Corners East
Suite A3
Norcross, GA 30071

Dewberry Designs
811 E. Highland Drive
Altamonte Springs, FL 32701
Phone (407) 830-6786
FAX (407) 831-0658
E-mail: dewberry@magicnet.net
www.onestroke.com

Index